W9-CMC-252

HUNTER MORAN HANGS OUT

ALSO BY PATRICIA REILLY GIFF

*Hunter Moran Saves
the Universe*

HUNTER MORAN HANGS OUT

Patricia Reilly Giff

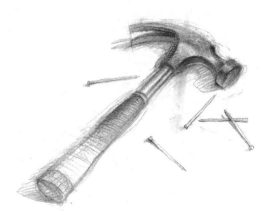

Holiday House / New York

Gloucester Library
P.O. Box 2380
Gloucester, VA 23061

Text copyright © 2013 by Patricia Reilly Giff
Art copyright © 2013 by Chris Sheban
All Rights Reserved
HOLIDAY HOUSE is registered in the U.S. Patent and Trademark Office
Printed and Bound in July 2013 at Maple Press, York, PA, USA
www.holidayhouse.com
First Edition
1 3 5 7 9 10 8 6 4 2

Library of Congress Cataloging-in-Publication Data

Giff, Patricia Reilly.
Hunter Moran hangs out / by Patricia Reilly Giff. — First edition.
pages cm
Summary: When neighbor Sarah Yulefski tells Zack and Hunter that she overheard
someone talking about plans to kidnap someone in their town, the twins use the last
four days of summer vacation to investigate.
ISBN 978-0-8234-2859-5 (hardcover)
[1. Twins—Fiction.   2. Brothers and sisters—Fiction.   3. Family life—
Fiction.   4. Kidnapping—Fiction.   5. Mystery and detective stories.
6. Humorous stories.]   I. Title.
PZ7.G3626Hth 2013
[Fic]—dc23
2013003172

To James Matthew Giff,
(and nobody else)
with love

DOOMSDAY...
MINUS FOUR

And right now we're trying to escape...

Chapter 1

. . . from Linny, who's screaming like a hyena. "Get back here, you two."

Just because she's the oldest, she thinks she's the alpha dog of the family.

"Arf, arf," I bark, pulling open the back door.

Linny's best friend, Becca, is standing right there. "How come Linny wants you?" she asks.

We don't bother to answer. Becca's the nosiest kid in the world, with a beak to match.

Mary bangs spoons on her high chair and gives us a toothless smile. "Bye-bye."

I wave at her and speed outside. Zack speeds with me.

"You left those disgusting things all over the kitchen," Linny goes on.

"Can't even leave one worm around," Zack mutters.

It's not quite one worm. We actually have a farm with about forty of them in the bottom drawer of the cabinet.

Terrific creatures. Highly intelligent. We're teaching

them to climb the table legs. Give them a boost and they're right up there, heading for the tabletop.

Unfortunately, two or three have wandered away. We're on a mission to find replacements.

"Hunter!" Linny screams. "Zack!"

Any minute she'll alert poor Mom. Without thinking, we take a shortcut across the front lawn, our feet sinking in a little.

We stop at the edge, realizing what we've done. It's a moment of horror. Our footprints zigzag across Pop's newly seeded lawn; it's as if something has chewed up the whole thing. Somehow we'll have to deal with it before Pop gets home from work.

In the living room window, our dog, Fred, with the skunk breath and nasty disposition, is doing somersaults on the back of the couch and yowling at the top of his lungs. They probably can hear him in Fiji.

Zack and I hit the sidewalk and keep going. It's a crucial getaway. We trot past the school; our classroom is on the second floor. That's Doomsday staring us right in the face. Four more days and we're prisoners again! Summer is disappearing fast.

Upstairs, Sister Appolonia is pasting moldy leaves on the window. In a flash, it comes to me that we're supposed to bring in last June's report cards. Impossible.

We buried Zack's with its horrific music mark in a pile

of garbage. Last time I saw mine, it was clamped between Fred's jaws. We told Mom the school is going green, saving paper, doing away with report cards. We'll tell Sister that Mom framed the cards over the living room couch.

Sister Appolonia spots us and sticks out her head. "How about a little help up here?"

"Sheesh," I mumble, but we maintain our speed. At the same time, I point up at a cloud. Let her think we've become deaf over the summer and we've taken up sky-watching.

We're about to cross Murdock Avenue when a head pops out from behind the telephone pole.

What next?

"It's Sarah Yulefski," Zack whispers. "Head for the woods."

He's right. There she is, Sarah Yulefski with her braces festooned with Rice Chex, and her knotty hair down to her waist. Sarah Yulefski, who told the whole class I'm in love with her.

I shudder, thinking about it.

"Stop right there, Hunter." She sounds like Alpha Dog Linny.

We dive out onto Murdock Avenue, but a truck barrels toward us, horn blaring, gravel spitting. We jump back, barely escaping with our lives.

"One of these days you're going to kill yourselves," Yulefski says.

If it happened four days later, it wouldn't be so bad. School would be closed on the first day for our funeral. We'd be heroes.

"Listen, guys," Yulefski says. "I have news."

Sure. She's playing in another concert. She has a new brown outfit for school that matches her teeth.

"Sorry," Zack says. "We can't stop. We're on our way to ..."

"...help Sister Appolonia," I put in.

Sarah Yulefski screws up her face. "You're going the wrong way."

I sigh. "All right, what news?"

She leans closer. "It's really bad. Terrible, as a matter of fact."

"I'm bracing myself," I say, and Zack tries not to laugh.

She takes her time, running her tongue over her teeth, dislodging a Rice Chex, twirling around to see if anyone's listening.

As if anyone in the whole world would be interested in what Sarah Yulefski has to say.

Wrong.

She leans forward. Whispers one word.

Zack's eyes are as big as pizzas and I can hardly swallow.

Chapter 2

"A kidnapping," Yulefski breathes. "It's going to happen right here in Newfield. Actually, it's someone..."

We lean forward, two inches away from Yulefski and her teeth.

"...in your family," she finishes, looking ecstatic at her bad news.

Zack and I stagger back.

"Give me a buck twenty-six," she says, "and I'll tell you the rest."

We dig into our pockets and come up with our life savings. Sarah Yulefski counts every penny, every dime, as if we were out to cheat her. "All right," she says at last. "The victim will fit in a cage." She frowns. "I think he said *thick*. A thick cage? Thick something, anyway."

"What? Who?" I manage. My legs are going to give way any minute. Zack sinks down on the sidewalk.

Yulefski holds up her hand. "I'm getting to that. I was hanging around in Vinny's Vegetables and Much More, listening to various conversations as I picked out bags of healthy snacks."

"Get to it, Yulefski," Zack says.

"Three things," she says. "Item one. The kidnapper was muttering to someone. Or maybe to him- or herself. I couldn't tell if it was a man, woman, boy, or girl." She shrugs. "It could have been an alien for all I know."

Zack cuts in. "Didn't you get a look?"

"I was in the beef jerky aisle," she says. "The napper was around the corner, probably looking at the cleavers on sale."

Cleavers!

"Item two. The kidnapper whispered that the victim never kept quiet for a minute. I think that's what he said; it was hard to hear. I had to poke my nose into all those packs of jerky."

I remind myself never to eat beef jerky for the rest of my life.

Sarah Yulefski runs her fingers through her knotty hair. "So here's the deal. I caught just a bunch of words: *Moran. Cage. Need thick? Thick money?*" She takes a breath. "Yes, he or she sounded like a foreign agent: *lure the victim in. Try not to get caught.*"

She works on her teeth. "You can see that. It would mean jail for the rest of his or her miserable life. You can't keep someone in a cage, throw him a little food once in a while..."

Zack makes impatient circles with his hands. "Keep going."

At the same time, I'm almost yelling. "Are you sure he said *Moran?*"

"One at a time here," Yulefski says. "And yes, I heard *Moran. M-o-r-a-n.* As for item three..." She looks embarrassed. "What was item three, anyway?"

Impossible.

She sucks on her braces. "Don't worry, it will come to me."

Probably two years after the kidnapper strikes.

Sarah Yulefski tosses her hair over her shoulder, just like *TV Witch Girl,* two o'clock, Friday afternoon. She disappears up the street.

Zack and I stare at each other. Should we head for the police station? Should we tackle Pop with the news?

Who'd believe Sarah Yulefski?

Zack reads my mind. "Only us, Hunter. Only us."

Chapter 3

We head for home without our life savings. Yulefski has no mercy. Not only is our family in terrible peril, but last week she charged us a buck seventy-four for our worm start-up.

But never mind that. We definitely have a kidnapping on our hands. Which one of us? I run through the whole family in my mind, oldest to youngest. Airhead William, Alpha Dog Linny, Zack and me, Mary, who almost lives in a high chair, and...

I stop dead in the middle of the street. *"The victim never keeps quiet."* Steadman shuts his mouth only to chew on the most unhealthy snack he can find.

Zack claps his hand to his head. "Small enough to fit in a cage. *A thick cage?*"

Steadman is only five years old. What a hole that would leave in our family. Instead of six kids, there would only be five, not counting the one that will be born any minute.

It's impossible to think about it.

We start to run and get as far as the front door. Linny, skinny hands on her hips, stands there with Becca, who's a mass of lumps and bumps. "Practicing gymnastics at Gussie's Gym," Becca says. "You should see the new guy, Alex. He's bent over like a corkscrew from working out."

I raise one shoulder. Who has time to think about Becca and her run for the Olympics, which will never happen anyway?

"You two are so lucky," Linny cuts in.

Lucky? I don't think so. "Where's Steadman?"

Linny waves her hand toward the house. "In the yard."

All fenced in. Safe for the moment.

"Here's your luck," Linny goes on. "Pop's not coming home for dinner."

Zack makes a Jell-O face, squishing his cheeks in and out. He thinks Linny has lost her mind.

I know she has.

But Linny points one finger at Pop's new lawn. "You'd better pray he doesn't get home before dark."

The lawn!

"I don't want to be in your shoes when he sees this," she says. "Shoes. Get it?" She snickers at her own joke.

"Hysterical," I say.

She opens the door, and Fred dashes out. He gallops toward us with a couple of frothy growls.

"Watch your ankles," Zack warns.

Becca jumps back and darts behind a tree. "That dog is a disaster," she mutters.

Steadman is coming out of the backyard. Clumps of

dirt cover his hands, his knees, his shirt. I don't want to think about what he's been up to.

"*Yabaloo!*" Steadman shouts.

Instantly Fred's mouth snaps shut; his tail wags. He's in love with Steadman. They disappear into the house with Linny and Becca right behind them.

We're left to see the mess we've made of Pop's lawn. "It's fixable," I say.

"How?"

"Sister Appolonia says there's a solution for everything."

But we don't have time to think about Sister Appolonia. We have to concentrate on salvaging Pop's lawn before he gets home, and then saving Steadman from a cage, thick or otherwise.

Zack snaps his fingers. "I've got it. Follow me."

We cross the street and walk along the weedy driveway of the empty house, until we hit the edge of Werewolf Woods. Huge trees. A muddy pond. Last year, Bradley, the neighborhood bully, with only three teeth, lisped that the pond was a bottomless pit and about forty kids had drowned in there. "Thaw a floater mythelf," he bragged.

Zack and I keep our distance from the pond and a possible appearance by Bradley from behind one of the trees, while I wonder if the kidnapper might deposit his victims in that murky water.

"Here it is." Zack points to a huge rock.

"What?"

"The gravestone."

I sink down on a pile of vines as he pats the stone.

"Don't you see? We'll roll this across the street and sink it right into the footprints. We'll tell Pop—"

I hold up my hand. I can see it. We'll tell Pop a coyote dropped dead in the middle of the lawn.

Excellent.

We get behind the rock. We shove it along, circling the trees, and rumble our way across the street, our arms and legs almost caving in.

"What else could we do?" Zack says. "Steadman crying. Fred howling from grief. The coyote too big to drag…"

"Actually," I put in, "the gravestone is quite…"

"…unusual," Zack says. "It adds pizzazz to the property."

We're totally out of breath by the time we get it in place. It looms up like a hundred-pound toad ready to spring. We're satisfied. The footprints are covered. There's only the trail the gravestone made as it wended its way over the lawn.

Unavoidable.

We head back into the house. Right now, we're on a kidnapper watch!

Chapter 4

It's dark by the time Zack and I head upstairs. Only one room has a view of the town and maybe the kidnapper skulking around.

William's room.

We unlock the three bolts and sneak in. We sneak quietly. If William finds us, it's goodbye. William throws a mean punch.

William is weird, anyway. He's painted horrible murals of Zack and me, both of us half-devoured by saber-toothed dinosaurs. He's painted the window, too: an orange planet, wet and sticky, heads for extinction in a black hole.

You can see out the window if you line one eye up tight against the exact center of the hole. There's a bare spot the size of a nickel.

Zack leans in, then draws back. "Dark as a cave out there." He looks like a Halloween pumpkin from the paint.

"We have to do something fast," I say a little desperately, "before Steadman is gone forever."

"And before Doomsday, when we're prisoners in room

213 with Sister Appolonia." Zack squints up at the ceiling. "We could sneak across to Werewolf Woods. There's a perfect view at night."

A voice cuts in. It's Steadman, standing in the doorway, wearing pajamas with huge holes in both knees. "You forgot. Poisonous snakes are curling themselves around the branches."

Zack and I glance at each other. We told him that last week when he followed us in there, talking nonstop around a Snickers bar.

"Listen," I tell him now. "It's deadly in there until the winter. You know, when it snows. The snakes hibernate like bears."

Steadman looks suspicious. "What about the perfect view?"

"I can't stand it," Zack says. "Didn't Mom put you to bed an hour ago?"

Steadman doesn't answer.

But wait a minute. Is that William clumping up the stairs? We dive out of there, the three of us, and head for Steadman's room, which is a minefield. Fred still isn't housebroken.

"Bedtime, guys," Mom calls from the stairs. "Love you."

"Love you, too," we call down.

I try a fake yawn. "Hey, Steadman, maybe I'll just lie on your bed." I stretch out on his quilt, away from Fred, who's walking around the edge on two back legs like a circus dog. His breath is extra foul tonight.

"I'm so tired I can't keep my eyes open," Zack tells Steadman. "Why don't you climb in with Hunter and get a good night's sleep? After all, kindergarten begins in a few days."

Huge mistake.

Steadman opens his mouth so wide you can almost see his big toe, and Fred tries to take a chunk out of mine.

"I don't want to go to kindergarten!" Steadman screams.

Zack looks at me. "Remember the kindergarten prizes?" he says over Steadman's yelling and Fred's growling.

"Hmm," I say, as if I'm trying to think. "An iPod? Someone got a motorcycle, I think."

Zack flips up the edge of the damp rug and lies on the bare floor. "Candy, barrels of it," he adds. "You could dive right in...."

"Orange slices," I whisper. "Hershey bars."

"I might try it," Steadman says. "For a couple of days."

Fred stops growling.

All is quiet.

Zack and I lie there for about seventeen hours, and finally Steadman closes his eyes. We count to one thousand to be sure he's asleep. Then we sneak out of his room and tiptoe along the hall, passing Mary's room. She's singing to herself in her crib. Mary makes a lot of noise, too. But she's safe from kidnappers. Mom watches her like a hawk.

We hop over the open paint cans in front of William's room, also a minefield, and we go downstairs, hardly breathing.

At the living room door, Zack and I give each other a silent high five. Pop is in his big chair, snoring like a rhino. He hasn't seen the coyote gravestone, or we would have heard about it.

What a surprise he'll have in the morning, I think uneasily.

Zack gives me a nudge. Inching its way across Pop's shoe is one of the wandering worms.

Zack dives across the room and grabs the worm just before it disappears into Pop's sock. Pop never moves. That's one great thing about him. When he sleeps, he really sleeps.

We deposit the worm in its home in the kitchen, sweep Mary's half-eaten toast crumbs off her high chair for a welcome-home dinner, and imagine the reunion the worms must be having as we slide out the front door.

Pop has forgotten to lock up again, very careless, especially when there's a kidnapper lurking around. We lock the door behind us even though it wouldn't keep a flea out.

Outside, we skitter across the street, circling around the light pole, and dart down the driveway of the empty house.

Strange, it almost sounds as if there are voices inside. But no time for that. We dive into the woods.

Way into the woods.

We just have to hope the kidnapper is staked out somewhere at the other end of town.

The trees are huge, higher than houses. Dive off one of those babies, and you'd be buried right there under piles of old leaves, muck, and maybe even snakes, poisonous or otherwise.

"This isn't going to work," Zack says.

"I know it. All you can see are tree trunks."

Zack looks up. His head is tilted so far it's almost leaning against his back.

I look up, too. I see the tallest tree in the forest, higher than St. Ursula's Church, but skinny as a stick.

"You know what we have to do," Zack says.

I have a sinking feeling. But he's right.

"We'll have to build a lookout tower," Zack says. "Up on top."

I can hardly see the top, but we can't worry about small details. Pop has rusty nails and pieces of boards all over the place.

I flex my muscles. We're ready to take action.

Chapter 5

We grab boards from Pop's shed and drag them behind us, leaving a dusty path in the street. Who knew they'd make so much noise?

We drop them under a tree, then go back to roll a barrel of nails into the woods. The nails are leftovers from Pop's plan to build a workroom before we were born. Now he's thrilled with his lawn seeding project. He'll never miss all this stuff.

In the woods, dark leaves and branches crisscross high over our heads. "Just like *Jungle Terror,* Saturday afternoon, four o'clock," Zack says.

There's nothing left to do but climb.

"Sheesh," Zack says. "Climb what?"

I see what he means. The lowest limb is almost out of sight. Even Pop couldn't reach it.

Zack throws his legs around the trunk to shinny up. He gets about two feet off the ground and falls back into an ooze of mud.

I'm not going to try that. Instead, we lean Pop's barrel

against the trunk and throw ourselves on top of the barrel. The cover sinks in.

Not only have I stabbed myself in a dozen places right through my sneakers, but we're still not high enough.

"Well," Zack says, yawning.

I hope he's going to say we'll forget about it for tonight. But no. He leans a board against the tree, backs up about ten paces, and takes off...

...through the ooze, onto the board, and he's right there, reaching, holding on to the lowest branch, swinging like a trapeze artist.

"Good effort," I say in a Sister Appolonia voice as he lands on a branch, legs dangling.

"Hand up another board," he calls down. "A good one for the floor."

I grab one that probably weighs as much as Nana and zigzag underneath, holding it high.

Zack leans over, a little too far. "Yeow!" He just avoids a major fall as he latches on to a branch. The board swings back and I manage to duck before I'm conked in the head.

We start over. This time he grabs the board. I put a couple of nails in my mouth and take off running, yelling, "Timber!" to man myself up.

Too bad about the nails. Once I open my mouth, all but one has disappeared into the undergrowth.

"Timber!" someone whispers back at me.

"Keep going," Zack calls down. "It's only an echo."

"I don't think that was an echo," I say. Halfway up, I hang on to the tree trunk. Back and forth, forth and back, until I'm dizzy. One way, I catch sight of trees with gigantic spider legs. I swing the other way. A killer snake reaches out to circle my ankle. "Poisonous!" I scream.

"A vine," Zack says.

I close my eyes. Insects buzz. The echo keeps ringing in my ears. *Timber.*

"Let's go, Hunter," Zack calls.

I lean my head against the trunk and open my eyes. Everything is still moving. "Onward to the next branch," I whisper.

Toward the top, the trunk is even skinnier. It bends, it sways. And we bend and sway with it.

"High enough," Zack says at last. "I can see St. Ursula's roof and the town round."

He's right. I spot the railroad station and Gussie's Gym. And there's the enormous Suicide Hill, which only the bravest skateboarders in the world would dare try.

Not me. Not Zack.

But we've forgotten something. Sheesh. The barrel of nails is all the way down below, and only one nail is left in my mouth.

"Don't worry about minor things," Zack says. "We'll lay the board out across a branch. You sit on one end. I'll sit on the other."

A balancing act. Good.

You can't beat Zack for brains.

But it's not so easy to keep the board steady. Zack scootches in on his side; I scooch out. It's windy up there, and the board seesaws. How can I search for a kidnapper if I'm trying to steady the board?

Wait a minute. I do see something. First I think it's just a shadow. My imagination.

But on the other side of the board, Zack gulps.

It's urgent that no one sees us. I duck behind the leaves, forgetting to balance the board and myself. The board tips toward me. I tip toward the ground far below. Zack is somewhere above me.

"Looook oooouuuut!" I shout.

I slide . . .

Fall.

The board snaps back.

We sail through the air, dislodging leaves and small branches.

"Yeooooowwwww!" I scream all the way down.

Across the street, Fred yowls, too.

Chapter 6

"I'm dead," Zack moans.

"You're right." I try to figure out if I'm breathing.

"Not even close to dead," a voice says. "Just scrambled brains."

The kidnapper? A female kidnapper?

I look up. Sarah Yulefski.

"I can't believe it." Yulefski, the echo I heard, the shadow I saw.

"Believe it," she says. "But I'm out of here. Your father's coming this way."

Yes, the front door is open, and Pop is coming down the steps. We must have made enough noise to wake the whole town. Leaves are still floating down.

I scramble up, searching for a place to hide. But Pop has eagle eyes. I watch helplessly. There's nowhere in the woods he won't see. Nowhere in town.

Of course he'll see us.

I hear Zack gasp. He knows it, too.

But no. It's something else.

Pop starts across the newly seeded lawn. "Sheesh," Zack says. "Pop doesn't see the coyote's gravestone."

There isn't time to yell *Watch out!*

Pop slams into the gravestone. He slides over the top and ends up draped over the whole thing, his head on one side, his feet on the other.

He's down.

But not dead.

His yowl is louder than Fred's.

"You'd better do something," Sarah Yulefski says over her shoulder as she heads out of the woods. "He's probably broken his neck."

At that moment, all the lights in our house go on. Shades snap up. Doors slam. Mom and Linny barrel down the steps and tramp over the new lawn. There isn't one spot left that's . . .

. . . . pristine, as Sister Appolonia would say.

They stop in front of the gravestone and lean over Pop.

Zack and I race across the street toward them.

"I knew it." Linny shakes her head so hard her hair flies. She points directly at us. "This is your work."

By this time, Pop is sitting up, leaning on the gravestone, yelling that both arms and one of his legs are broken.

I have a quick picture in my mind. Zack and I will have to wheel Pop around in Mary's stroller for the rest of his life.

"Can you walk, John?" Mom asks calmly.

"Of course I can walk." He sits up against the grave-stone.

"Whew," I whisper.

Pop waves one of his broken arms around. "The lawn is ruined. And how did this rock get here in the middle, anyway?"

"It's a gravestone," I begin, but suddenly I have major doubts that our coyote story is going to work. Besides, Linny opens her mouth, ready to give us right up.

Now Steadman is at the door. "Something's buried there," he says around a caramel pop. "One of those huge tannish"—he snaps his sticky fingers and squints up at the light over the front door—"with horrible teeth."

How did he come up with that?

Spying on us, of course.

Pop hobbles into the house, holding on to Mom and Linny. "I'll get to the bottom of all this in the morning," he says.

"Wicked bad news," Zack whispers to me.

But then...

...over my shoulder...

I look across the street at that gloomy empty house.

Wait! Is there a light flickering inside?

Wait again! Down at the end of its weedy driveway where the woods begin, I see a shadow again.

A huge...

Someone?

Something?

And it's definitely not Sarah Yulefski.

Zack turns to see what I'm looking at. "It's worse than a coyote," he says.

There it is, a terrifying clue.

The kidnapper is hanging out in the empty house...

...spying on us.

On Steadman.

We dart into the house behind the rest of the family, almost knocking Linny over as we head for our bedroom and lock the door behind us.

DOOMSDAY ...
MINUS THREE

But we may be doomed early ...

Chapter 7

It's morning. A red-hot sun beams through the window. Outside, something is banging.

Is William bouncing his basketball against the house? *Boom-ba. Boom-ba.* No. It's *swish-a, swish-a.* He's painting something.

I stretch, wondering why I feel uneasy. Maybe it's because I had a nightmare; it was something to do with books.

Something I'm supposed to remember?

But what?

Everything that happened last night comes back to me: kidnappers and gravestones. In one move, I'm out of bed. At that moment, footsteps pound down the hall, straight for our bedroom.

Pop's footsteps, heavy as an elephant's.

Zack pulls the pillow over his head. "It's time for the gravestone inquisition."

But Pop keeps going down the stairs. The whole house vibrates. "This is it!" he yells.

Zack leans up on one elbow. "Pop's leaving home, and it's all because of us."

Mom's footsteps come next, a little slower, a lot lighter. She opens our door and smiles at us. "We're on our way to have the baby. Nana will be here to take care of things in an hour or so."

Nana. Terrific.

Mom frowns a little. "Pay attention to Linny in the meantime."

"Have a boy," we call after her, crossing fingers and toes.

"Think of names," she calls back.

We don't have to think. We've figured it out already. K.G. for Killer Godzilla. We'll tell Mom it's for Kevin George, or something regular like that.

The banging goes on. It sounds as if it's coming through the window. The day has a whole new look, though. Nana will cook for hours, humming, patting our shoulders as we go by. She hardly remembers who's who. We can search for the kidnapper in peace.

Except for Linny. She bangs on our door with both fists. "Let's get this house cleaned up before Nana gets here," she says. "The whole place is a mess because of you guys."

She's got to be kidding. Nana loves to clean.

I pull a T-shirt out from under the bed. DON'T WORRY is splashed across the front in huge red letters. I'm worried. We have two days to solve this kidnapping.

Zack and I go down the hall. We pass William's room. Mom says he has a head on his shoulders. Too bad there's nothing in it. A huge Gussie's Gym bag is on the floor, probably stuck to the new paint. He said he paid Gussie a fortune for it. That means ten bucks, at least.

Airhead William.

We peek in at Steadman. He's fast asleep with his thumb in his mouth and a half-eaten Baby Ruth bar melting on his pillow. We peek quietly, though. Once he's up, we'll have to follow him around all day to be sure he's safe from the kidnapper.

For once Linny is right. The kitchen is a mess. She's standing at the sink, bubbles piled high, dishes piled even higher. "Grab a towel," she says over her shoulder.

"The dishwasher's still broken?" Zack asks.

"What do you think?" she says.

"I think you're doing a terrific job, Linny," I say. "Just keep an ear out for Steadman while you're at it, will you?"

We dive out the door and stand on the back steps, listening. "Is that noise coming from Werewolf Woods?" I say.

Zack looks across the street. "I think so."

I can hardly hear him. Linny is screeching at us from the kitchen. It sounds as if she's being dragged away by the kidnapper.

Who'd want her?

"Close the window," Zack calls in to her.

Surprisingly, she slams it down, yelling something about a pile of books on the hall floor that anyone can fall over.

Books! Last night's dream! Something floats into my mind, then out again.

Linny presses her nose against the glass. "What about those worms?"

"Don't worry," I call back. "They're healthy. They won't catch anything from you."

We grin at her to show we're joking; then we concentrate on the noise coming from the woods.

"The kidnapper is building a prison, right there in the middle where the vines are thick," Zack says.

"Easy for the kidnapper, just steps away from the empty house where he's hanging out," I say.

In front of the house, we try not to look at Pop's ruined lawn with the gravestone looming up in the middle.

We zigzag across the street, heading for the woods, and take a shortcut along the driveway of the empty house. Strangely, there are shades on the window. Black. You can't see an inch inside, even though we take a couple of jumps to look.

"Crummy house," Zack mutters.

Even William's painting would be better than the peeling wood. Perfect for a kidnapper.

In the woods, we pass Pop's barrel of nails. Some of his wood is missing. Now the kidnapper is turning into a thief.

The noise is closer, earsplitting. We look up.

And up.

Whatever is there is well hidden. We walk around the trees, squinting. I can see a couple of boards at the top of one of the highest trees.

A lookout tower? It slants to one side, as if the whole thing will topple over any minute.

Sarah Yulefski leans over the edge. She's mostly hidden by the leaves. It's an improvement.

"Excellent view from up here," she calls down. "I built it wide so there's plenty of room."

Zack and I shrug. Should we build a platform of our own or become partners with Sarah Yulefski? Either option wears me out.

Zack leans closer. "Isn't that our wood? So that makes it our platform."

"Hey, Yulefski, where'd you get the wood?" I yell up, trying to remind her that she's actually a thief.

"Some idiots left it here," she says. "Most of it was rotten, anyway."

I open my mouth to tell her it's our property, but what's the use? We don't want the whole world to hear that we're the idiots.

"Want to join in?" she asks. "A buck a day."

"You're crazy," Zack says.

"Listen," she says. "This was a tough job. I had to get my brother, Jerry, to help. We used ropes and—"

"All right," I say. "We'll just have to owe you."

I hear footsteps and look over my shoulder. Bradley the Bully is coming along, muttering to himself.

Most of the time, he hangs out at Gussie's Gym; he wants to be a world champion wrestler someday. What he doesn't have in teeth he makes up for in muscle. He could probably take Sister Appolonia right now.

I heard her call him devious.

Devious is right. He has a Vinny's Vegetables shopping cart in his garage filled with potato chip bags and weight-lifting stuff. Probably all stolen.

Get too close to him and he wraps one beefy arm around your neck until you beg for mercy. Zack and I scramble up the tree like a pair of mice escaping from a fox and throw ourselves onto the platform. It rocks a little, then settles back.

Yulefski has outdone herself.

A pair of binoculars hangs from a rotten branch above. A notebook hangs from another branch. Two thick books rest on the edge.

Yulefski has a pencil behind each ear. "If you're going to observe," she says, "you have to take notes." She points down as Bradley passes by underneath.

He never looks up. He goes straight to the pond.

"He might even be the kidnapper," I say.

"I never heard of a twelve-year-old kidnapper," Zack says. "He can't even drive a getaway car."

Yulefski reaches for her binoculars. "You have to look

with one eye," she says. "I cracked the other lens over my brother Jerry's head." She draws in her breath. "I can't believe it."

"What?" Zack and I say together. But I don't need binoculars to see what Bradley's doing.

He's poking around in the pond with a big stick. And what does he come up with?

"Is that what I think it is?" Zack forgets to whisper.

I swallow. From here it looks like a head of hair, curly, dark, swamped with muddy water.

I remember what Bradley said that time, "Thaw a floater mythelf."

Never mind a world champion wrestler. He's turning into a murderer.

I lean a little too far over to watch. Yulefski's books topple over the end of the platform and crash onto the ground below.

Chapter 8

We lie on the skinny planks, hardly breathing. With one eye, I peer between the spaces and catch a glimpse of Bradley down below.

He looks around, squinting. One huge hand is closed in a fist that would knock your teeth out. The other holds the stringy hair up high.

Is there a head attached to that hair?

If not, where is the head?

Yulefski opens her mouth. "I'm not afraid of him, the big bully. *Ya-ya!*" she shouts.

They can hear her in Timbuktu, wherever that is. She's going to get us killed.

Across the street, Fred begins to yowl and howl.

Bradley turns and starts toward our tree.

But someone else is yelling; it's Linny, screeching again. "I'm coming after you!"

Bradley stands frozen for about a quarter of a second; then he throws the hair over his shoulder into the pond and lumbers out of there.

Zack gives me a high five. "Good old Linny after us again," he says.

"Bradley's nothing but a sniveling coward." Yulefski grins. "I read that in a book."

I close my eyes for a second. Who can bear to look at those teeth of hers? That snarly hair?

She slides off the edge of the platform and wraps her legs around the tree trunk. "I have to get my books. Wait until Sister Appolonia hears I've read forty-two this summer."

It hits me hard.

No wonder I had that nightmare. We were supposed to read three books this summer, then write essays on how they changed our lives.

Zack realizes it, too. He looks as if he's going into a coma.

Linny yells again. "I'm not fooling. Nana's here, and lunch is ready."

Hand under hand, we climb down the tree and jump the last hundred feet or so. The shock of it goes from my toes straight up to my head.

Yulefski's waiting for us, rubbing the mud off the book covers. "Mrs. Wu at the library will have a fit if they aren't in good condition," she says.

"See you when school starts," I tell her. "Or maybe around Christmas."

Nana's car is in the driveway, a tomato-red Caddy, probably as old as she is.

Linny's still yelling. And is that her friend Becca chiming in? Becca who's one big black-and-blue mark from working out at Gussie's Gym?

Halfway down the street, Yulefski adds to the screeching. "I just remembered the third thing about the you-know-who."

We stop dead.

"Hunter? Zack?" Linny screams.

Another clue. Terrific. "See you right after lunch," I tell her.

She blows breath through her braces. "Dr. Diglio, the dentist, is seeing me after lunch. I'll catch up with you."

"Can't you just tell us now?" I ask.

But Yulefski's into suspense. "See you later." She skips up the street.

We head for home. Zack is still chewing over the book situation. "How are we going to read three books in a couple of days?" he moans as we gallop along. He takes a massive jump from the edge of the lawn to the coyote gravestone, and then to the front path.

He snaps his fingers. "Suppose we make the whole thing up?"

"No good. Sister Appolonia has probably read every book in the world. What else does she have to do?"

Nana's in the kitchen. She gives us a hundred hugs. Even with a face that's a little cracked, she's not bad-looking, and she gives out the best birthday presents in the world. Too bad she's hoping the baby will be named after her. Maizie. I can't think of anything worse. "It's a boy," I say, to let her down easy. "K.G."

She tilts her head.

"Kenneth Gerard."

She smiles, then mixes us up as usual. "Your teeth are really straightening up nicely, Zack."

They're my teeth, and Dr. Diglio says I'll be lucky if I don't lose them by the time I'm twenty.

Who'll care at that point?

We slide into chairs around the table. Becca sits across from me, going on about gymnastics and Olympics and how she's going to sacrifice everything to win a medal.

She frowns. "I just need to get six bucks to pay Gussie's Gym for the next couple of weeks."

Linny picks the weirdest friends.

One time, Zack and I sneaked up to Gussie's window to watch. Diglio the dentist was doing push-ups. If I had matchstick legs like his, you'd never catch me in a pair of shorts. After two push-ups, he collapsed on the floor, ready to pass out. Or pass away. Sister Appolonia had to stop swinging from bars to help him lean against the wall.

Nana dishes out melted-cheese sandwiches, burned around the edges. Her cooking tastes like Mom's. She turns to Zack. "I've made your favorite lunch, Hunter."

We both hate cheese.

Actually, it's William's favorite. He loves burned stuff.

Mary hangs out of her high chair by the straps, dropping cheese all over the floor. Lucky Mary. She does whatever she pleases.

Becca goes on. "I've already earned two You Did the Best You Could medals." She raises her arms over her head, congratulating herself.

Next to her, Zack looks grossed out.

"Here's mail." Nana dumps it on the table. As if any of us would be getting something. It's always junk: advertisements for steaks, a furnace, and life savers for a swimming pool, which we do not have, even though we've asked for one for our double birthday every year. We'll try Nana again in November.

But here's something new. A letter addressed to Mom, which looks a little odd.

Weird, as a matter of fact.

Huge letters in red read: PRIVATE! PERSONAL! READ IMMEDIATELY!

Could it be from the kidnapper?

Mom's mail is sacred. But poor Mom is in the hospital having Killer Godzilla. Checking out that mail is the right thing to do. But not in front of Nana, and definitely not in front of Linny.

I slide the letter off the table and shove it into my back

pocket. I tear off the black edges of cheese and stick them in there, too.

Linny has eyes like a hawk. She stares at me as if I've just committed a major crime.

Zack leans under the table; he's going to get rid of some cheese. Fred eats anything. But Zack comes up looking uneasy. "Where's the dog?"

I look around. Never mind Fred. What about Steadman?

I push my chair back from the table so fast it falls over. A piece of cheese is a lump in my throat. I talk around it—actually, I'm almost screaming. "Where's Steadman?"

William with an empty head on his shoulders looks under the table.

Nana clutches her throat.

But Linny sits there calmly for a change. "He's on the living room floor asleep, with Fred."

I sink back in the chair until my heart gets started again. Zack does the same thing. "Can you imagine..." He doesn't finish. He can't get the word *kidnapper* past his lips.

I think of the letter in my pocket. I tilt my head toward the door to let Zack know we have to get out of there.

"Thanks, Nana," I say. "That cheese sandwich was the best."

"Yeah," Zack adds. "You ought to be on one of those TV cooking programs."

That's going a little too far. Nana looks at us suspiciously.

"Want us to help clean up?" I know she loves to do dishes, even without the dishwasher.

"Aren't they great!" Nana tells Linny and William.

Mary spits out her cheese.

Then we escape. We trot around the side of the house. It's a mess, filled with weeds and junk. No one can see it from the street, so Pop has let it go back to nature. At least, that's what he says.

Fred loves it. He likes to roll around in the smelly weeds, looking as if he's in heaven. We sink down in Fred's heaven, weeds to our eyeballs.

I hold up the envelope, then run my finger under the seal, so slowly we could be there all afternoon. We'll lick the whole thing back together afterward. No one will ever know that we had a first look.

Excellent.

"Let's ask Nana for a fingerprinting kit for our birthday," Zack says. "Genuine. Police type."

I nod. We can put the pool idea aside until Christmas.

"Yeow!" Zack yells. *"Bees!"*

I jump, ripping the whole envelope open, and the letter flutters away in a couple of pieces. "Are we dead?" I yell.

Zack is swatting his head, dancing around; then we're out of there.

But not before I get a quick look into the living room window. No one is asleep on the floor. Not Steadman. Not even Fred.

Chapter 9

We dart around the side of the house and nearly knock Becca over. "Great lunch," she says, "if that dog didn't keep going for my shins." She rubs her leg. "Have to get to Gussie's Gym. The new kid, Alex, is waiting."

"Go for it," Zack says.

We barrel through the house, yelling, "Steadman! Fred!"

In the kitchen, Linny is telling Nana that we're operating on half-cylinders.

We race through the living room and peel off to take the stairs two at a time.

Nobody.

Nothing but a crumpled-up Hershey bar wrapper on Steadman's bed.

"Stolen from me," Zack says.

We head for the basement, even though we know Steadman wouldn't set foot down there. We've told him an alligator lives in the furnace room.

It's probably not true, but you never know. We saw that on *Would You Believe?* Monday, 6 AM.

Zack and I clump down loudly. We make noises deep in our throats to terrify the maybe-alligator.

The light at the bottom of the stairs is out again. When I'm grown-up and rich, I'm going to have a guy work for me; he'll do nothing but change lightbulbs every two minutes.

We trip over a ratty old rug that Mom calls an antique and crash into Pop's tools. Pop says he's building a retreat for himself down there. Zack says it's more like a dungeon.

"Steadman," I whisper. "Where are you?"

We stand absolutely still.

Steadman doesn't answer.

Fred doesn't growl.

We do hear something. What? We don't wait to find out. We race up the stairs and out the front door and sink down on the steps.

There are no two ways about it. Steadman has been kidnapped.

"What should we do?" I ask Zack.

"We can't tell Nana," he says. "She'll drop dead of a heart attack."

"William is useless," I say.

"And Linny will never believe us."

"She will if she can't find Steadman." We poke our heads in the front door. "Hey, Linny."

"She's out back somewhere," Nana calls.

We dash around the side of the house, through Fred's oasis, and into the yard. Linny is leaning against the playhouse. And she's holding...

Holding...

"The kidnap letter," Zack says.

And that's when Linny begins to scream at the top of her lungs.

Linny loves Steadman. We all do. This is the worst thing that's ever happened to us. Steadman won't even make kindergarten. "I'm glad that at least he had that Hershey Bar," Zack says over Linny's yelling.

We go over to her. With both hands she's ripping up what's left of the letter.

"Stop!" Zack sputters. "Are you demented?"

We dive for it, but Linny dashes around the playhouse. We tackle her, and the three of us crash into the birdbath, which is more muck than bath.

A thousand pieces of the letter float over the yard, some of them caught in Pop's half-dead rosebush, most of them covered with mud.

Linny is still screaming.

"We're going to get Steadman back," I tell her as Zack crawls around, gathering up microscopic pieces of paper.

"Steadman?" Linny yells. "Steadman?" Her face looks

like a purple eggplant. Skinnier, though. "What are you talking about?"

"You don't know? Steadman's been kidnapped," I say. "And the letter is probably the ransom note. You never should have ripped it up. We need all the clues we can get, and we have only..."

"...two and a half," Zack puts in.

Linny sinks to the ground, getting more purple by the second. "I knew it. You have the brains of mentally challenged fleas."

I shake my head. What am I missing here?

"It's a ransom note, all right!" Linny screams. "But I'm the one. Me. Not Steadman. I'm going to be kidnapped any minute."

Zack holds up his hand. "What did the note say?" He's calm. Intelligent. Right to the point.

We lean forward. Linny runs her pretzel-thin hands over her face. "Some of it was ripped up already."

Zack and I look at each other, remembering the bees.

"I couldn't stand reading the rest of it," she says. "Once I saw *one million dollars* and *ransom...*" Her lips quiver. "Once I saw *Lin...Mor...*"

She sinks down on her knees. "Linny Moran. My name. I'm the kidnappee."

I swallow. The kidnapper thinks Linny is worth a million bucks? Amazing. "Are you sure you didn't see Steadman's name?"

She takes a ragged breath. "Piles of paper are still float-ing around. They probably want him, too."

Poor Pop. Where will he get a million dollars to pay the ransom?

And Linny, bent over, moans: "I should have listened to Sarah Yulefski."

Chapter 10

Linny is part of this family, I tell myself. What would Mom do without her? Somehow we'll have to save her, and Pop's money.

"Sarah told me the kidnapper wants to keep a kid in a cage. A kid who never shuts up. A kid who'll fit..." Linny holds out her arms, skinny as strings. "That's me. Linny Moran."

She looks furious. "But my conversations are right on. Dynamic. Even Sister Appolonia said so."

I cut in. "How much did you pay Yulefski for her information?"

"What are you talking about?" she says. "Nothing."

Great. And we paid a fortune for the same thing.

Linny looks around. "What will I do?"

"You could hide in the basement while we figure things out," Zack says.

She shudders. "There might be an alli—" She breaks off. "Not the basement. No way."

"The attic," I tell her, hoping she won't remember the colony of dive-bombing flies and hanging wasps' nest up there.

Linny glares at me.

"How about the bottom kitchen drawer?" Zack's getting impatient. "Pull out the pots and pans and slide right in."

I wiggle my fingers, trying to remind him about the worm farm with the apple cores for their treat.

But I'm getting impatient, too. There hasn't been a sound out of Fred all this time, a lifetime achievement for him, not a somersault, a backflip, or a walk on two back legs. I almost miss him.

And poor Steadman, who loves to talk, might be gagged and blindfolded, just like the kid on *Terror in the Night*, Wednesday afternoons, one o'clock.

"Linny, dear," Nana calls from the kitchen.

Linny looks toward the house, head tilted. "I'm locking all the doors and windows. Then I'm hanging out with Nana until Mom and Pop get home with Peaches."

Peaches? What is she talking about?

Zack knows. "K.G.," he mutters.

I nod at Linny. "Nana's your best bet with those fat grandmother arms. Great for protection."

We watch as Linny dives around the side of the house

and slams herself inside. Then we take another minute to gather up the scraps of the ransom letter. Later, we'll put them together like a jigsaw puzzle.

"Now what?" Zack asks.

"The lookout tower," I say. "Steadman has to be somewhere. We'll keep an eye out all over town." This is the worst. The kidnapper might be after our whole family.

We dash across the street, then hesitate. A van is parked in the driveway of the used-to-be-empty house. The van is the worst mess I've ever seen, probably smashed up in about forty accidents. We tiptoe around it. The hood is up, showing innards that are rusted together.

"That baby belongs in a junk heap," Zack says.

We keep going into the woods and begin to climb. The tree shakes and bends with our weight. I reach the top first. My head is almost level with the lookout tower, and . . .

"Look out!" Zack yells.

Conk!

Something hits me in the head.

I manage to hold on with one hand. "The kid-napper!"

Zack grabs my legs to steady me, the two of us diving backward.

"Hunter!" a voice calls. "Is that you?"

Fred begins to bark insanely.

I scramble back up and onto the platform. Steadman is crouched at one end, waving a thick branch around like a sword.

The branch that nearly knocked me unconscious.

Fred is at the other end, growling, showing his wicked-looking teeth. Steadman leans toward him, hand in the air. "*Yabaloo,*" he says fiercely.

Fred's mouth snaps shut.

Zack throws himself down on the cracker-thin edge of space that's left. "What's that about?"

"Fred doesn't know English," Steadman says. "I'm teaching him a new language. *Yabaloo* means 'Be quiet, for Pete's sake.'"

Fred's eyes bulge with the effort to keep his snout closed. But you have to hand it to Steadman. *Yabaloo* works.

Zack hangs on to the inch of board that's holding him up. "What are you doing here?"

"Don't move too much," Steadman says. "Whoever built this thing didn't do such a hot job."

"Steadman, pay attention." Zack has no patience left. "We've been searching all over the place for you."

Steadman looks off into the distance. "Someone has to look out for the kidnapper."

"How do you know about that?" Zack asks.

Foolish question. Steadman knows everything, and he's only five.

Steadman looks worried. "I think someone is ready to steal Joey."

I don't even know who Joey is. But I'm feeling such relief over finding Steadman without a gag and blindfold that I'm willing to let Zack do the inquisition.

"All right," Zack says. "Who's—"

Steadman doesn't let him finish. "You don't even know your new baby brother?"

Zack slaps his forehead. "What makes you think...?" he begins, but Steadman isn't paying attention. He's feeding gummy bears to Fred. That's all the information we're going to get out of him.

So, holding on to a branch overhead to steady myself, I check out the whole of Newfield. I see Becca at the town round. She's racing along, heading straight for the bench donated by the town fathers.

"Go, girl!" I hear her yell to herself.

She raises one leg, and then the other...

She's up, but not over.

Her feet catch on the top of the bench, bending like noodles. She hangs there for a second, then disappears into the sticker bushes behind the bench.

Behind her, some kid, with a mop of dark hair and a pair of knees like cantaloupes on toothpick legs, tries the same thing. We hear him yell as he lands headfirst in the sticker bushes with Becca.

I turn. Bradley the Bully, muscles bulging, is coming out of Vinny's Vegetables and Much More.

Wait a minute. I nudge Zack. "Someone's walking up the driveway of the used-to-be-empty house."

"Get a look at that guy," Steadman says. "Huge."

I lean forward. The platform shakes. But the guy has disappeared inside the house.

Next to me, Steadman is pulling on a rope.

Where did that come from? Something's attached to it.

I lean out an inch.

It's a basket.

"Now what?" I ask.

"Simple," Steadman replies, and yells, *"Vestibulia!"*

Before our eyes, Fred clambers over us and into the basket.

"You don't think he climbed up here all by himself?" Steadman says, as if we're the five-year-olds.

Steadman lowers the basket. It's a good thing Fred weighs only four or five pounds. The basket bangs against the tree all the way down. Fred looks terrified.

"Ecobeko!" Steadman yells down as Fred reaches the ground.

"That means two things," Steadman says. " 'Good dog,' and 'Don't move an inch until I get there.' " With that, he climbs down out of the tower. We watch him carefully, every step, until he and Fred reach the house and march inside.

Safe!

At that moment, there's a huge crash, almost like an explosion, that comes from the direction of the used-to-be-empty house.

Chapter 11

"Something's going on over there," Zack says. We climb down the swaying tree like a pair of monkeys heading for a banana festival and stop short at the end of the weedy driveway. The junk-o car is gone, which is a good sign for us.

Still, we try for an invisible look. We scrunch our heads into our necks, bending over to minimize ourselves as targets. Then we sidle up to the house. The shades are down to the sills; not a slit of light shows through.

We trot around the entire house; it's closed tight as a clam. Here's a criminal who doesn't want the world to know what he's doing. What *is* he doing, anyway? Blowing up his victims?

We spot the cellar stairs. That's probably where the action is.

We start down the worst steps anyone could imagine. Old leaves are gunked up in piles.

And is that...

"A mouse," Zack says. "Dead as a doornail."

We jump over the step, just missing the poor guy's tail.

There's no shade on the cellar window. We give each other a high five...

...and peer in.

It's dark as a tomb.

"That's where he keeps his victims," Zack says. "No doubt about it." He reaches out to try the doorknob.

"Don't even think about it," I begin, but I never get to finish.

Yeow!

The kidnapper crouches over a table near the window. He has a saw in his hand, but we can't see what he's amputating.

His hair hangs down over his eyes, but you can still get a look at them. Blazing eyes like the ax killer in *He's After You*, Tuesday night, midnight, which we're not allowed to watch.

The napper looks up. "Hey!" he yells.

We don't answer. I'm paralyzed, my tongue glued to the top of my mouth.

And there's the explosion again. It's the junk-o car coming up the driveway.

We take off. We don't even worry about stepping on the mouse corpse. We keep going at a hundred miles an hour, around the car, across the street, and sink down in Fred's oasis, trying to catch our breath.

"That was a close one," Zack says after a minute. "The

kidnapper was two inches away from us. No wonder he wants a million bucks ransom. The first thing he needs is a new car."

I nod absently. "Was that a kid in the basement?"

Zack makes a Jell-O face. "A dangerous accomplice."

So now it's two against two. I try not to think of how pathetic that is. Zack and I are like a pair of ants looking up at gigantic shoes coming down, ready to stamp us out.

We sit there thinking. "Maybe we'd better find out Yulefski's third clue," I say. "We'll have to get our evidence all set before we go to the police."

Zack nods, and we're off looking for Yulefski. She's not hard to find. She's curled up on her front steps, reading a book. It must weigh a thousand pounds.

"The clue?" Zack asks, wasting no time.

Sarah closes her book. "I almost saw the kidnapper's hand. Well, maybe a finger or two."

"What about the rest? The face, for example?" I sound like *Great Detective Mysteries,* off the air now.

She waves her own hand impatiently. "I told you I was in the beef jerky aisle; the kidnapper was in cleavers." The book slides out of her lap and lands on the step. *Make the Best of Your Beauty.*

Sheesh!

"The kidnapper dropped a cleaver or something," she says. "I bent down. I could just see the edge before a hand snaked out and grabbed it."

"That's it?" Zack says. He's furious.

She looks up at a squirrel darting around in a tree.

"Focus," Zack says.

"There was something about the fingers."

We lean forward. She leans back.

"Chopped off?" I ask.

"Giant sized?" Zack asks.

"Wearing a watch?" I add.

She holds up her book. "That's the thing. I can't remember." She raises her shoulders. "I'm thinking about it. I'll let you know as soon as I . . ."

I can't believe it.

We don't wait to hear the rest. It's time to check out the ransom note.

Chapter 12

We go back into the house, stopping to scoop up a lonely worm and drop it into the farm with its buddies. We drop in a handful of dirt, too. Worms are crazy about dirt. We pass Nana, who's stirring some kind of brownish pudding in a pot, and Steadman, who's asleep under the kitchen table.

Nana glances over her shoulder and smiles at us. "Your father called. Things are coming along. Maizie will be born soon."

William stands behind her, painting the tabletop a violent shade of green. Wait until Pop sees it.

William squints over at Nana. His entire face is spattered with green polka dots. "It'll be a boy," he says. "We'll name him Leonardo, after that artist."

Sheesh.

Even Nana looks dazed.

Steadman's awake now. He follows us up the stairs and down the hall to our bedroom. "I'm teaching Fred to walk on two legs," he says.

"Great," Zack says absently.

"Hey," a voice whispers as we pass Linny's room.

I see a long, skinny braid, almost like the mouse tail on the used-to-be-empty cellar steps. It snakes out from under her bed.

"Don't worry," I tell her. "We're on the case."

But we have no time for Linny. "Great hiding place," Zack says, and we keep going.

As we reach the top step, there's a huge bang. We stop dead in our tracks. This time we know where it's coming from. We dive over to the window.

The beat-up car is pulling out of the weedy driveway, muffler dragging, sending up sparks as it zigzags down the street.

In back of us, Steadman yells something like *"Lumba-comba!"* Fred hauls himself up on his front two legs and takes a couple of steps. *"Notobado,"* Steadman says, and peels off into his bedroom.

Zack and I close our own door and sit against it. This is a moment for privacy. We can get down to business.

I turn my pockets inside out. A hundred bite-sized pieces of paper drift onto the floor. Most of them are covered with burned cheese. We'll have to put the whole thing together like a surgeon sewing on a head or a leg.

We fiddle with the papers, pushing them around on the floor, trying to make sense of them.

There's a capital *L: Linny,* of course. And more than one *S.* Could it be *Steadman?*

Sure.

But here's something else. Zack gets a whole sentence together. Almost, anyway.

WANT TO LOOK...

"Like the son of Frankenstein," Zack mumbles.

"Yes. Friday night, nine o'clock. Taking a lizard and turning it into..."

Zack and I stare at each other, horrified. Suppose the kidnapper wants to turn Linny into a lizard?

"If we got her back," Zack says, "she'd have to live with the worms and eat paper and lettuce leaves."

"Ridiculous," Sister Appolonia would say.

Sister Appolonia! That reminds me: three books in three days! Three essays!

I squint up. "*Frog and Toad* changed my life. I am now interested in aquatic wildlife."

Zack glances over at me. "You're in sixth grade, Hunter. Sixth!"

"We'll have to pick up some books at the library," I say. "Skinny as possible."

"Didn't we do that in the beginning of the summer?"

Right. Whatever happened to them? Mrs. Wu is going to have a fit; they'll be overdue about two months' worth.

And we don't even have enough life savings for the overdue fines.

There's no hope for it. We'll have to (a) find them or (b) face Mrs. Wu at the library for another pile. I'm wrung out just thinking about it.

I lean forward, looking at the rows of words Zack is arranging.

What pops up is the word *KILL*.

This is worse than kidnapping. Much worse.

But wait. Arrange some letters differently, and you get *cell*...And another few: *others*. "Others in the cellar?" I yell. A chill runs through me, even though it's about ninety-eight degrees in the bedroom.

"We have to get down into the cellar of the used-to-be-empty house," Zack says. "Free those victims before..." He runs his finger across his throat.

I shake my head. I can barely go down into our own cellar with that maybe-alligator lumbering around in the dark.

"This is the perfect opportunity," Zack says. "We know the kidnapper isn't there. He's just driven off in that piece of junk."

"Suppose he comes back," I begin.

Zack puts on an irritable face. "You heard the sound of that car. Don't you think we'll know when he pulls into the driveway?"

"And what about the accomplice?"

"Two against one," Zack says.

We pass Linny's room again. I don't even see her braid. Then we head across the street to the empty house and maybe the end of us.

Chapter 13

We go straight to the back of the used-to-be-empty house and peer down the cellar stairs. We know what we're doing now. We avoid the mouse corpse and peer in the window.

Yes, there's the table and the saw hanging next to it.

Zack turns the handle. The door swings open.

"That's trespassing," I say. "We can't go all the way in."

Zack nods. "It's kind of a surprise, though. If we can get in, why can't the victims get out?"

"They might be handcuffed," I say. "Or foot-cuffed."

I shield my eyes against the cellar darkness. What do I see? Boxes. Shelves with books and papers piled high.

I lean in a little farther. I don't see the step in front of me until it's too late. *Oof!* I'm down on the cement floor, setting off a gong that's so loud my ears ring.

I sprawl there, frozen, trespassing. Next to me, Zack is frozen, too. The whole neighborhood probably heard that.

"A bell," Zack whispers from the steps. "Just a bell. A huge bell. Nothing to be afraid of."

I'm afraid. I'm definitely afraid.

We hear a creak upstairs, over our heads. And then there's another.

"Someone's up there," Zack says. "Get up. We have to get out."

I peer at the narrow stairs leading to the killer's lair. It's a repeat of *Nest of Aliens*, Wednesday afternoon, four o'clock.

The door opens and here comes the kidnapper.

I'm stuck. Why can't I move?

My T-shirt is caught in the door, my ankle in the bell rope. I kick my leg free and grab the edge of the shirt, pulling it almost free. A huge chunk of it is still imprisoned inside.

The kidnapper clumps down the stairs.

Poor Mom. Zack and I will be gone forever. And there're still Steadman and Linny to worry about.

Zack pulls me, yanks me by the hair, the neck, wherever he can reach.

I'm scrambling backward. I see the dangerous accomplice looking down.

He yells. I yell. And then I'm free. Zack and I race down the weedy driveway as I hold what's left of my T-shirt together. We don't stop until we've gone all the way to the end of the street.

We sink down in the alleyway between the library and Vinny's Vegetables and Much More. Next door, Yulefski is bent over backward, heading up the library steps. She's holding a pile of books that go from under her chin to her knees. No wonder Sister Appolonia thinks she's a star.

"Wasn't there a book we read a long time ago?" I snap my fingers. "Maybe we could use that for a report. You know, it was about three animals who got lost. One was a dog, one was a tiger, maybe. Or was it an antelope? Something like that."

"A cat," Zack says. "And we saw it in a play. The whole school saw it. Sister Appolonia loved it."

I raise my shoulders in the air. We'll really have to read.

"No more than seventy pages," Zack says.

"Fifty," I say, and we haul ourselves up the stone steps and into the library.

Mrs. Wu is at the desk, talking to someone about old cars. A huge someone with hair the color of Nana's pudding.

From the back, he looks familiar. He turns, but I don't have time for more than a quick look. Zack is dragging me away, down the aisle, around the corner, into the biography section.

He leans against the bookshelves. "Did you see?" He sounds as if he's strangling.

And then it comes to me. Talking to Mrs. Wu, standing right out in the open, is the kidnapper. I look around. No, the accomplice isn't there. He's still in the used-to-be-empty house guarding victims.

"Oh, the brazenness," Zack says. That's Sister Appolonia's favorite word.

We hear those footsteps, *clunk, clunk*. He's in the next aisle.

Zack leans forward into the shelf. About twenty books crash through to the other side, probably landing on the kidnapper's foot.

It doesn't bother the kidnapper. He's talking to someone. "Are you here all by yourself?" he asks.

That's the most dangerous thing I can imagine a kidnapper asking.

I peer forward, but I can only see feet: the kidnapper's, probably size 100 workman type, and the other, a little kid's sneakers. They look familiar, almost like my old ones.

Zack is clutching me, but I'm trying to see. Yes, they're really my sneakers. I recognize the hole in the toe. They're the ones...

The ones...

"I'm looking for my brothers," the little kid says. "We're on the trail of a kidnapper."

Steadman! He's crossed Murdock Avenue by himself, the busiest street in town, and now he's having a conversation with the most dangerous man on the East Coast.

"My dog's outside," Steadman goes on. "He's not allowed in the library."

"What kind of a dog?" the man says.

"Pretty vicious. He gave my sister's friend, Becca, a bite she'll never forget. I'm the only one who knows how to handle him."

Zack and I stare at each other, making motions. What to do?

We have to be brave. We have to act fast. We take a deep breath; then we march around the side of the book stacks to confront the kidnapper and pull Steadman away before it's too late.

And that's almost what we do. We don't confront the kidnapper, we don't even look at him. We grab Steadman, pick up a couple of books that are lying on the floor, and head out.

"See you," Steadman says to the kidnapper.

And then somehow I feel courage welling up in my chest. "I know what you're up to," I call back over my shoulder. "But we're watching you."

We don't wait to hear what the guy says. It's only two steps to the door.

But Mrs. Wu is tapping her fingers on her desk. "The books," she says.

I look down at the pile in my arms. I don't even know what I'm doing with them.

Mrs. Wu is frowning. As Sister Appolonia would say, she's a no-nonsense person. She looks at us over her glasses. "You have to sign them out."

Sheesh. As if we'd steal these babies. They weigh as much as I do.

I put the pile on her desk. I look over my shoulder to see if the kidnapper is coming, but he's nowhere in sight.

Mrs. Wu is nodding. "Excellent choices here." She looks down at us over her glasses. "You also have six books out all summer. It's going to cost."

"Tomorrow," I say. "We're going to bring them right back."

I don't stop to see what excellent choices we have. I take Steadman's hand, and the three of us are out the door.

Chapter 14

In the backyard, Nana barbecues hamburgers, with a little help from Linny and Becca. Becca's going on about the new kid, Alex, who's building steps for their workout practice. "Olympics, here we come," she says.

Linny's nodding. She looks a little rumpled from lying under her bed, but she's prepared. She's got Steadman's looks-like-real sword tucked under her jeans belt and William's baseball bat against the picnic table an inch away from her.

A worm is wandering around. One of ours? Sheesh, all that guy needs is a sunburn. I scoop him up, take a chunk of hamburger, and rush them both into the house.

I'm no sooner outside again than Linny begins. "I want some help after supper." She stares at Zack and me. "We're going to string spoons and forks over the back steps. The front steps, too."

Zack shakes his head at me. This whole kidnapper thing has sent her right over the edge.

"Maybe William can help," I say.

Gloucester Library
P.O. Box 2380
Gloucester, VA 23061

"Yeah," Zack adds. "He can paint the spoons and forks."

William gives Zack a nasty kick. "I have better things to do," he says.

And then a surprise. "I'll help," Nana says, dishing out some of that brown pudding, which turns out to be butterscotch, the stick-to-the-roof-of-your-mouth kind. "But why, Linny?"

Linny takes a blob of pudding and swallows it down. "I hate to tell you this," she says, "but there's a kidnapper in town looking for a victim. All the evidence points to me."

Nana bites the side of her lip. I can't tell if she's trying not to laugh, or if she's worried. "We'd better get that silverware up, then."

Linny nods. "If the kidnapper bangs into them, it will make enough noise to wake the neighborhood. I'll be ready to dial 911."

"Don't worry, I'll help," Steadman says.

Great. That will take care of him for an hour. We're free.

Linny starts to gather up spoons. It gives us a great opportunity to get out of there without finishing the pudding, and without having to hang silverware all over the property.

We slide out from the picnic table, and Mary waves bye-bye from her high chair. It's her best trick.

We stop in the kitchen to check on the worms. A couple are twirled around, heads or tails poked up out of the dirt. They look comfortable and happy. Good.

We head for the lookout tower. It's getting dark now, and the insects are going wild.

A couple of problems. Yulefski is there ahead of us. We can see her legs dangling from the platform. Bradley the Bully is sloshing around in the edge of the pond, fishing for something.

"What to do?" I whisper.

"Climb quietly, that's what," Zack whispers back. "We have no choice. We'll have to watch the kidnapper's house. If he comes out, we'll follow."

We take running jumps. Hand over hand we climb. We check to be sure Bradley hasn't seen us.

Yulefski looks up from her book. "Everything's quiet all over town," she says.

A moment later, the door to the used-to-be-empty house flies open. The huge hulk of the kidnapper comes out and barrels up his driveway, his sneakers, elephant sized, pounding against the cement.

We don't stop for a breath. We dive down the tree, the branches swaying as if we're in a hurricane, and barrel after him.

He crosses the street.

It's our house he's after.

But no, he doesn't even give it a glance.

We see him passing the streetlight. A moment later, he crosses Murdock Avenue and goes in through the gates of the town round.

Mom would be there, walking with Pop, if the baby, K.G., weren't on his way.

The napper's heading around the round now, just like a regular jogger, but he doesn't fool us. He turns, and we dive into a bush. Has he seen us? It's entirely possible.

Footsteps come up behind us now. The accomplice? I swing around, ready to defend myself, who knows how?

"It's Yulefski following us," I say.

"Hunter," she says, hands on her hips, elbows like coat hangers. "Have you gone crazy? What are you two doing in the bushes?"

Zack gives her a *zip the lip,* and I pull her into the bushes, whispering furiously, pointing to the kidnapper, who's coming around our side of the round. "Do you want the kidnapper to hear? He's already sent us a ransom note. He really means business."

She frowns. "The only way to see the kidnapper is from the lookout tower." Then she stops, mouth open. She points at the kidnapper.

She bends over, hands on her knees, laughing through those disgusting braces of hers. "You think he—" She breaks off, trying to catch her breath. "That he..."

"Spit it out," Zack says.

She shakes her head. She can't talk. And here comes the kidnapper.

I try to cover her mouth, a little too hard, I guess.

She yells, *"Ouch!"* The kidnapper hesitates, then keeps going.

"You think...," she begins again, and shakes her head. "What a pair of idiots. While the kidnapper is roaming free in town, you are chasing the new principal of St. Ursula's School."

Chapter 15

How can I sleep? We've yelled at the new principal, we still haven't tackled the summer reading, and worst of all, we're being menaced by a kidnapper we still haven't found.

Weighty, very weighty.

But I have to sleep. It's the only way out.

And so the room is pitch-black and the pillow is jammed over my head when I hear Linny screaming down the hall.

Fred is barking, growling, howling.

In one motion, I'm out of bed. I grab one of the library books; it's the heaviest thing in the room. Zack's out of bed, too. He's holding the lamp over his head, the wire trailing.

Zack's eyes are like pizzas in the darkness. "We can do this. We have to save our sister."

What is it she's shouting?

We tiptoe to the bedroom door and ease it open. We have to surprise the kidnapper. It's our only hope.

"Peaches!" she shouts above Fred's horrendous noise.

Peaches?

Fred grabs the lamp cord and shakes it so hard that Zack drops the lamp on my foot. The lamp is in a thousand pieces; I'm lucky my toes are still attached.

Now I hear Nana. Is she yelling, too?

William's door bursts open.

Steadman is standing against the wall, thumb in his mouth, shaking his head. "A girl," he says. Then he's really awake. *"Yabaloo!"* he shouts.

Fred snaps his jaw shut.

"Yes!" Linny stops in her tracks, dancing around, arms out, hitting the wall. "It's Peaches."

"Maizie," Nana breathes, her hair twisted up in rollers, her face full of whitish cream. She smiles at us. "Your father just called with the news."

A girl.

This is the latest in a string of disappointments. And poor Mary, asleep in her crib, doesn't even know she's not the baby anymore.

Still...

Zack and I grin at each other. We've had an alternate name plan just in case this happened.

We all troop downstairs to the kitchen. Nana pulls out a container of milk and a box of saltine crackers. She puts an open jar of peanut butter in the middle of the table. A knife sticks out of the top. William's work. He never puts anything in the dishwasher.

I sit and chew; lights are blazing in the used-to-be-empty house. We've probably awakened the whole neighborhood. Worse, we may have awakened the kidnapper, wherever he is.

After we finish off the crackers and milk, everyone goes back to bed. Everyone except Zack and me.

Upstairs in our bedroom, we look through the pile of books. Not one under a hundred pages; the letters are so small I'll be wearing an eye patch by the time I've finished the first chapter.

"What we could do—" Zack holds up his hand so I don't interrupt. He picks up the skinniest book. "One hundred two pages." He snaps his fingers. "What's half of that?"

I squint up to the ceiling. "Forty-one?"

"Fifty-one." He squints, too. "You'll read one half, I'll read the other. We'll figure out two life changes." He looks thrilled with his idea.

We're both yawning now; I can't keep my eyes open. It must be after midnight. We'll tackle fifty-one pages in the morning.

But Fred is barking again, a muffled bark.

Where is that coming from?

"It doesn't sound as if it's in the house," Zack says. He goes to the window and peers out at the backyard. I look over his shoulder.

Is that Fred out there? We don't see him, but he's howling like Dracula.

How has he gotten out of the house?

We see the falling-apart playhouse we built with Pop a couple of weeks ago, and the half-dead bushes with their withered leaves dragging on the ground.

"Why hasn't someone watered all that stuff?" Zack asks.

I don't remind him that Pop told us to do it about fifty times.

But now we see something else. Someone is in the yard. It looks like an old man, all bent over, wearing one of those hats with brims that cover his eyes. His nose is huge, hooked like a pirate I read about once.

He's dragging an odd-looking striped bag behind him. It's big enough to stuff Linny inside. In the dim light it seems to move, to bulge one way and then another.

Without thinking, I shove up the window. "Hey!" I yell.

The guy, whoever he is, looks a little familiar. But before I can get a good look, he backs out the gate and takes off.

We're going to take off, too. We can't let him get away with this.

We won't bother going through the house. Nana sleeps with one eye open. Instead, we dive into the closet for one of those rope ladder things. Nana gave it to us; she's afraid of fire the way Linny is afraid of kidnappers.

"Just throw this thing out the window if necessary, then climb down," she told us. "Read the instructions. It's easy as pie."

We haven't read the instructions. And it's not easy as pie.

The thing is heavy, but we manage to loop it over the windowsill, the handles like claws, ruining the paint, but no one will notice; the whole room is chipped from our wall-walking in spikes last summer.

I go first. I climb out backward, the ladder swaying like the lookout platform. I look over my shoulder at the maybe-kidnapper, who's rushing down the alley.

"Hurry!" I yell to Zack as I find places for my toes. This ladder was built for feet like Mary's.

Zack backs out behind me.

The kidnapper looks over his shoulder, too . . . and trips over his feet. *"Oof!"* he yells.

I leap off onto the ground, but my own feet are caught; the ladder comes with me, and Zack lands on my head.

Never mind that my brain is scrambled. We untangle ourselves and go after the kidnapper, kicking the rope ladder away.

Too bad we've forgotten sneakers. A thousand stones with sharp edges are hanging around. We dance down the alley on tiptoes and zigzag across Pop's lawn again. We'll have to deal with that later. A hyena memorial, or a grand WELCOME HOME, K.G. sign.

But right now, we're saving lives. Our family is depending on us.

Ahead of us, the kidnapper sprints across the road, passing the streetlight. I know who this is; I'm sure of it. If only I could figure it out.

And what about that bag that seems to have a life of its own?

"Wait up!" I yell.

He doesn't wait; of course he doesn't.

We hobble over the curb, but here comes a delivery truck with a huge picture of bread on one side. Too bad the side's a little dented. The bread looks squashed.

We have to wait until it lumbers past. And even losing those seconds makes us lose the guy.

Which way has he gone? Into the woods? Down to the town round? Maybe he's racing to catch the midnight train to the city.

We look back and forth, toward the library, then the used-to-be-empty house, and the dark and creepy Werewolf Woods.

The guy has disappeared.

There's nothing more we can do tonight. We head for home.

DOOMSDAY ...
MINUS TWO

And we're toast....

Chapter 16

It's morning. My head hurts, and the soles of my feet are torn up, but Mom and Pop are home with the new baby. We gallop down the stairs to see her.

The baby's face is a little red, a little squashed, and she looks like William, poor kid. She howls like Fred.

Mom sinks down with her on the big chair in the living room. Pop leans over them. He doesn't seem to realize that the baby isn't going to win any beauty contests. He looks thrilled. Good. It will keep his mind off the chewed-up lawn.

I reach out and the baby curls her fingers around mine. She belongs to us. I'm really glad she's here. I'm glad Mom's home, too.

Nana holds on to Mary, who's jammed half the couch pillow in her mouth. "Do you have a name for her?" Nana asks Mom, and crosses her fingers.

"Peaches," Linny whispers.

"Joey," Steadman says.

"Leonardo." William stands two inches away from the baby. "She looks like me."

Nana's eyes widen.

"She certainly does not," Linny says.

Zack and I cross our fingers. "What was your grandmother's name?" I ask Mom, knowing very well what it was.

Nana and Mom say it at the same time. "Kathleen Grace."

We nod.

They smile. "That's a beautiful name."

"Kathleen Grace," Nana breathes. "My mother's name. How perfect is that!"

"Great idea," Pop says.

Linny's lower lip is out a mile. "I'm still calling her Peaches."

"I'm calling her Joey," Steadman says.

"We could even call her K.G." Zack and I give each other a high five. *Killer Godzilla.*

The baby opens one eye and squints at me. It's almost as if she knows Zack and I have railroaded the family into her name, but she doesn't mind.

"Wait until Fred sees her," Steadman says. "He's going to go bananas."

"Where's Fred, anyway?" I ask.

Steadman looks around. *"Komazahere!"* he yells. He's

so loud, the baby stops crying and blinks. Mary knocks over a vase on the table and begins to chew on a daisy.

Fred doesn't *komazahere;* he doesn't even bark.

The doorbell rings. Becca is here to see the baby. She looks as if she's jumped off a ten-story building into a pile of cement.

"What happened?" Nana asked.

"Gymnastics," Becca says absently. She stares at the baby. "She seems a little squashed."

"She does not," we all say together.

"Nicely squashed, I mean," Becca says.

"Komazahere!" Steadman screams. He runs through the dining room, into the kitchen. "Maybe he forgot the language," he says over his shoulder. He clatters upstairs, and we clatter behind him.

"Fred, you're the best dog!" Steadman cries. "Come out wherever you are."

I'm beginning to have terrible thoughts. Last night in the dark. Chasing the maybe-kidnapper. The bulging bag.

Fred has been taken away in that bag.

Fred, who never keeps quiet.

Fred, who'd fit in a cage.

Fred, the kidnappee!

Not Linny, not Steadman, but still...

...part of our family.

Zack's eyes bulge. He's figured it out, too. He looks

at me and shakes his head. We're both thinking the same thing. This is the work of a madman.

"Fred," Linny breathes from behind us. "Who'd want Fred?"

Steadman opens every closet door, every dresser drawer. He's crying so hard he can barely get the words out. "He's a great dog. I bet he's been kidnapped. He's worth a hundred dollars at least." He cries harder. "I have only three quarters and fourteen pennies to get him back."

"Hunter and I are rich," Zack says. "We have money tucked away all over the place."

Actually, we have less than Steadman. But we're on our way to deal with the kidnapper. Somehow.

"Don't worry," we tell Steadman. "We'll come back with Fred."

Chapter 17

Outside it's almost too hot to move, but we drag ourselves to the town round, whistling for Fred. Zack even tries a *"Komazahere"* or two.

But Fred doesn't *komazahere*.

We try every street in town. We see a couple of dogs panting in the shade, but not one that looks like Fred, with his weasel face and his sharp teeth.

We sink down on a bench; we're so tired we ignore the pigeon goop. "Why did we bother to look all over the place in this heat?" Zack moans. "We know he's been kidnapped, probably turned into hot dog meat by now."

I think of Steadman's sad face, his tears. He's such a great kid. And then I remember the bulging bag last night. We know that bag. It's a Gussie's Gym bag. We look at each other in horror.

William?

"One of those bags was in William's room," Zack says.

I can hardly get the words out. "William's the kidnapper?"

William has gone crazy.

"I thought it was an old man," I say. "All bent over and wearing that hat."

"It could have been anyone. Almost anyone," Zack says. "We just have to hope it wasn't William."

It feels as if it's 100 degrees; the sun is burning a hole in our heads. Still, we haul ourselves to our feet and head for Werewolf Woods. We'll try the lookout tower next.

The woods are shady, cooler, the insects loud. We can't find our tree. How is that possible?

"It was this side of the pond, right?" I ask Zack.

"I think so," he says.

We wander this way and that way, and then we circle the muck at the edge of the water. Something is floating in the center. It looks like one of Pop's old boards.

We glance up at the trees. A board dangles from a skinny branch. Heads back, we zig zag underneath; we step on bent nails and a couple of boards that are sinking into the weeds.

The lookout tower is gone; the whole thing is torn apart. "I can't believe it." I kick at one of the boards. "Bears, maybe."

Zack makes a Jell-O mouth. "It wasn't a bear. This is the work of the kidnapper. He's afraid we're getting too close for comfort."

I look around uneasily. "What's that?" I say.

Not far from Pop's floating board is a bunch of brownish hair. What did Bradley the Bully say?

"Dead bodies," Zack mutters.

We stare at the hair. Stare hard. Could it be poor Fred? My heart stops beating.

Zack clutches my arm. "We have to go after him, give him a decent burial."

"We'd need a boat," I say.

Zack shakes his head. "No good. There's no time to build one."

I slap at a mosquito, staring at the pond, trying for inspiration.

"I've got it," Zack says. "Pop's old boards! We could build a raft."

I've said it a million times. You can't beat Zack for brains.

"Actually..." He squints out at the pond. "We don't even have to go that far. We can each take a board, straddle it, and paddle out with our hands."

I make my own Jell-O mouth. "Are you sure the boards will hold us up?"

I don't want to remind him that Bradley said once that the pond is miles deep. I don't even want to remind myself that I'm not the greatest swimmer in the world and Zack is worse.

Zack, the thinker, points. "Don't you see that board of Pop's in the center?"

"It's floating, all right," I say. "At least half of it."

"So what's your worry?"

I'm filled with worry. I don't even know where to begin. Instead, I check out boards under one side of the tree; Zack tackles the other side. Most of the boards have nails poking out like porcupines; a few would snap in half even if Mary tried to ride them. "I guess this isn't going to work," I say, almost relieved.

"Don't worry," he says. "I've got two perfect ones right here."

They don't look perfect to me. But Fred's out there, *a floater*, as Bradley would say, and already I'm planning the perfect funeral.

Chapter 18

We throw our sneakers under the tree, then pick up the boards. Like a pair of ponies, we gallop to the edge of the pond and belly-flop in.

We're soaked in muddy water in two seconds, but Zack is right. The boards seem to be holding up well underneath us.

Something slithers behind me in the murky water. It's long and narrow: a snake, of course. William collected them until Mom said they might be poisonous. This one certainly looks poisonous, with its slippery yellow back. Maybe it's a python.

I'm glad we have only a collection of worms.

I don't want to get my hands too close to the snake, but I have to paddle. I dip in two fingers and try to push the water away from me. The snake speeds after me as if we're having a race.

It's winning.

This may be the worst thing that's ever happened to

us. I glance back at the water's edge. How did it get so far away?

I look down at the snake. He seems to have grown in a minute; he's almost as wide as my wrist. "Snake!" I yell, to warn Zack.

Up ahead, Zack is having his own problems. He seems to be much lower in the water than I am. The board has disappeared, and so have his legs. He looks as if he ends at his waist.

I paddle faster to catch up to him.

He's paddling faster, too. But now I can't even see his waist. He ends halfway up his orange T-shirt. But it isn't orange anymore; it's mud color.

And something else. I seem to be riding lower in the water, too.

"We're sinking!" I try to turn. I paddle with my hands, my arms; I seesaw my legs back and forth. The water churns underneath me.

I'm disappearing into the water. Never mind the snake. I'll be drowned before he can take a bite out of me.

And there goes Zack. He's finished. "Goodbye, brother!" I yell.

He gurgles something back.

And then he's gone. All that's left is the top of his head, covered by a smear of muck.

I'm next. I take a last look at the pond. We're dead center. Pop's floating board is a foot away; so is Fred's corpse.

Bradley is going to be thrilled.

I'm dead. Not breathing. Coughing. Sputtering.

Arms over my head.

Legs kicking.

And then I'm up.

Really up.

Standing up.

Pop's boards pop up, too.

How can that be, in this bottomless pond?

Next to me, Zack is standing, blinking water out of his eyes.

The water is only up to our middles.

"What's the matter with that Bradley, anyway?" Zack reaches down and splashes up some of the water with his hands to clean his face.

Not much better.

I don't even bother. We have to scoop Fred up and get out of this pond before a nest of snakes descends on us.

And that's what we do. We take a few steps, mud squishing between our toes. We reach out and pull. Fred doesn't come up. He's really in there solid. A pain right to the end.

I give another yank. And something comes up. But it's not Fred. It's a pile of reeds, or weeds, or something. A pair of snails hang on to the roots; so does a stringy snake.

"Not Fred after all," Zack says. "This whole thing has been for nothing."

We stagger out of the pond, leaving Pop's boards to

float around by themselves. We throw ourselves down in the mud around the pond and take a few breaths. What next? I count on my fingers. We still have to find Fred, then the kidnapper...

Could it be William?

Then read three books that will change our lives.

"Our lives *need* changing," Zack says, reading my mind.

It's too much to think about.

I hear the sound of skateboards on Suicide Hill.

Things could always be worse.

I lie back and close my eyes.

Chapter 19

We slog our way across the street, dripping muck and weeds. I use my hands like windshield wipers, back and forth across my cheeks, my forehead, my eyes.

Behind us, someone is laughing like a maniac. I don't even bother to turn around. It's Bradley the Bully, of course. He must have watched the whole not-nearly-drowning event.

Forks and spoons clink on bushes. Pop holds his head. "Some idiot is stringing pots and pans all over the backyard, and..."

He waves his arm at the dangling spoons in front of him. "I don't know how we'll cook tonight, how we'll eat." He breaks off. "What have you two been up to now?"

"Um...," I begin.

Pop comes down the steps. "I don't even want to know."

It's a good thing. I'm too worn out to make up a story. What I'm going to do is rinse myself off and lie on the grass for an hour before I begin to check out the kidnapper with the Gussie's Gym bag on his back.

But no. Pop has other ideas. Saving the family is not an option.

"Clean yourselves up," he says, "and then we're going to turn this lawn over and reseed the whole thing."

Inside, Mary is banging the last spoons around, and K.G. is screaming at the top of her lungs. We can see Steadman out the back window. He's all right, hammering at the falling-apart playhouse, trying to shore it up.

"How about William for the lawn instead of us?" Zack asks.

"William!" Pop slaps his forehead. "William! He's in the kitchen clearing the green glop off the table."

It's really not great when Pop takes a day off from work. If only he'd relax, enjoy the end of the summer.

He forces a smile. It's because Becca has just arrived. "Hi, Mr. Moran." She looks a little uneasy. "I hear Fred has disappeared."

"What next?" Pop says, kicking at the monstrosity monument.

"It's much more peaceful without him," Becca says. "I'm Fred's target. He barks, he growls, he chews my leg. Not a very nice dog, right?"

But Steadman has appeared in front, his eyes red. "We have a gravestone for one animal," he says. "We'll have to get another one for my poor Fred."

Zack and I give Becca a look of disgust. But now she's telling Steadman that he can always get another dog, not one that froths at the mouth and turns backflips over people's feet.

I turn to Steadman. "We're going to find Fred, don't you worry."

"I'm really worried," Steadman says.

I'm really worried, too. But as soon as we reseed the lawn, we'll be hot on the trail of the Gussie's Gym bag. How many people could have those bags? Five? Six?

Along with William?

We're sure to track Fred down.

I pat Steadman's shoulder as Zack and I head for the hose around the side of the house. It's all in a mess of plastic loops, spurting water from a dozen leaky places. We hold the end over our heads, but almost nothing drips out of the nozzle.

But now another problem. Sister Appolonia is coming down the street, like a battleship pulling out of the harbor, all engines blasting.

There's not even time to disappear.

She stops. "Congratulations on the new baby," she tells Pop. She looks at the lawn. "A problem." She glances at us. "Good thing you have plenty of help."

"It's the help that ruins everything," Pop says.

From the corner of my eye, I see movement across the street. It's the used-to-be kidnapper's accomplice. He's hanging over the junk-o car engine, its innards spread over the driveway, peering out at us.

But what is Sister Appolonia saying? Something about books, of course.

Pop is nodding.

"I guess you haven't seen a book in their hands all summer," she says.

"Their books are all over the place," Pop tells her. "Eight or nine, at least. I fell over a pile this morning."

Sister looks surprised, more than surprised. She looks shocked.

Zack and I give each other invisible high fives.

Still looking at the kid across the street, Sister says, "Then I have very good news for you. Gussie's Gym is giving bags out all over town so kids can carry their books to school." She nods. "A generous woman. She's giving them to the parents, too."

Forget the high fives.

We now have about a hundred suspects!

And if that isn't enough, Sister Appolonia puts her hands on our shoulders. "Please plan to spend the day with me tomorrow. I need last-minute help. We can talk about all you've read while we get things going in the classroom."

I can't believe it. There's no peace in the whole world. Even Doomsday is moving up. We might as well throw ourselves back into the mud pond that doesn't even cover our heads.

Chapter 20

We're on our way to Gussie's Gym, mushing ourselves along, every muscle pulsing from working on Pop's lawn—actually, Pop's dirt; there's no lawn left.

The job isn't finished. We've just left Pop banging things all over his toolshed, searching for the bag of grass seed. We could tell him it's gone. We thought it would be perfect for worm farm food, but no, Yulefski told us worms aren't crazy about grass seed. And then a stiff breeze came along. Seeds flew all over the neighborhood, probably stopping to grow at every house but ours.

But why upset Pop with that news? We'll buy him tons of grass seed as soon as we get money for our birthday next year.

We pass the bottom of Suicide Hill. My head is almost worn out, too tired to crane it back to see the top. I don't have to look, anyway. It's implanted in my brain, a mile high, at least, all cement; it shoots almost straight down to the other side of the railroad station.

You'd have to be crazy to try it.

High up, someone is skateboarding down now, zigzagging back and forth, speeding along at a hundred miles an hour, ready to kill himself. I can't help watching.

A helmet covers his head; his arms are curved up and out for balance, his dark hair streaming out in back. He's screeching something at us.

Not a guy after all.

It's Sarah Yulefski!

I close my eyes.

"She'll be dead any minute," Zack says. "Sister Appolonia will be devastated."

Yulefski cups her hands around her mouth and almost rams the side wall. *"Folllllloowwww meeee, guys!"* she yells.

She zooms around the curve and heads toward extinction in front of us.

We sink down in the weeds, probably poison ivy, maybe poison oak, and watch for the crash. "Sit here for a few minutes," I say. "I don't want to see her corpse."

There's no crash.

She's survived.

"Let's get out of here before she catches us," I say.

We scramble up and walk toward Gussie's Gym. Across the way, the six o'clock train is steaming in. The noise is unbearable. So is Sarah's screech. *"Hurrrrrrry uuuuppppp!"*

We hear another voice, almost as loud. "Wait up, guys!"

It's Steadman.

Sheesh.

"You're not supposed to cross the street," Zack tells him.

Steadman holds up three fingers. "Three streets." He screws up his face. "No, maybe it was four."

We can't even tell him to go back home. It would be our fault if something happened to him. I shudder to think about it.

Steadman shakes my arm. "Why are you hanging out here? There's no time to lose with the kidnapping on our hands." He hesitates, mouth quivering. "It's snack time. Fred likes to eat up in my bedroom. A couple of pretzels with those dots of salt all over them. He loves stale potato chips, too." He begins to wail.

My ears are ringing. "Fred will be back in no time."

Yulefski's waiting for us, helmet hanging from one arm. She doesn't even have a scratch. She's in better shape than Becca, the Olympic gymnast. "It's about time you got yourselves here," she tells us. "There's something we have to do right away."

Zack tries to say something.

She cuts him off with a slash of her hand in the air. "Listen." She jerks her head toward the long yellow building in front of us. "We have to investigate Gussie's Gym. But we have to do it quietly. Gussie's a mean one when it comes to intruders."

I notice that Gussie doesn't take great care of the building. Great big strips of yellow paint are peeling off the cement blocks. The windows are streaked with a century of dust.

Sarah's right about Gussie's nasty disposition. William said one time that it's almost as bad as Fred's.

If it weren't for Steadman...

Where is Steadman, anyway?

I twirl around. Zack twirls around. Steadman's nowhere.

But he's somewhere, all right. I catch a glimpse of the bottom of those sneakers with matching holes. He's climbing into the filthy basement window of Gussie's Gym.

The window slams shut behind him.

I push at it; no good. I can see through a small hole in the glass that the lock has snapped shut.

He's locked in. We're locked out.

"Wonder how far he had to drop?" Yulefski says.

My heart is stopping again.

Yulefski swishes air through her braces. "We can go right through the front door. Ask if there are any..."

"...bags left," Zack finishes for her.

Gymnasts are coming through the open doors now, ready to collapse from their workouts. There's Mrs. Wu, wearing workout clothes in a horrible shade of orange. William would love it. Dr. Diglio staggers out behind her, knees knocking, looking as if he'll faint any minute.

We push past them, like salmon going upstream the wrong way.

More gymnasts push past us.

Gussie is sitting at the desk, her hair piled high in a nest that could house a couple of good-sized sparrows. She doesn't look thrilled to see us. "Closing time," she mutters.

In back of her, taped to the wall, are a thousand messages. KEEP FIT is one, with a photo of someone with muscles like Bradley the Bully. There's an advertisement for perfume that looks vaguely familiar, and cutouts of dogs, cats, and something that looks like a walrus. JOIN THE CONTEST, GYMNASTIC PETS. HUGE PRIZES.

"Register tomorrow," Gussie says, snapping a piece of gum. "Six bucks."

"I have only a buck twenty-six so far," Yulefski says. "And the one-seventy-four worm money."

Zack nudges me that it's our worm money. We'll never see any of it again.

"We were wondering about bags," I say, hoping Gussie won't notice that Yulefski is inchworming herself across the floor to peer into the gym.

Yulefski takes a final hop to check out possible kidnappers on the balance beam or the basketball court, or doing sky-high jumps on the trampoline.

How obvious is that? She's like that evil spy from outer space on *Deadly Worlds,* Thursday morning, seven o'clock.

Gussie taps her pen on the desk. "Time to leave. Six bucks tomorrow," she repeats as if we haven't heard.

I eye the basement door. Still no Steadman. And no Fred, of course.

"How many bags did you give out?" Zack asks Gussie.

"Excuse me?" she says, as if it's none of our business.

I think fast. "We might do an article for the school newspaper about your generosity."

Gussie pulls a couple of bags out from under the desk and hands them to us. "Don't forget to spell my name right. *G-U-S*..."

"Rhymes with *fuss*," Yulefski says, back at the desk.

Zack cuts in. "We need a list of all the people you gave bags to..."

"...so generously," I add.

Gussie looks as if we're crazy. "Who knows?" She shrugs. "Does that make a difference in the article?"

"Probably," Zack says.

Gussie looks irritated, or maybe disappointed. She jabs the pen through her hair nest. If there are sparrows in there she's probably stabbed one.

Yulefski reaches out to pinch Zack's arm.

"No, I mean, we'll try for a bang-up article," Zack says. "We'll just hang around awhile so we can describe the place. Give you lots of credit."

I nod, acting excited about the article. It's too bad Sister Appolonia canceled our newspaper last year. She said it was a disgrace, that we'd spelled fifty percent of the words wrong and the content was dismal.

"Come back tomorrow," Gussie says. "You can look around. I'll tell you all about our good work. I'll even give you a gymnastic discount. Five dollars and ninety-five cents."

Yulefski is eyeing the door to the basement, too. It's a thick door, metal.

It stays closed.

Is Steadman caught down there? Crying? Screaming? No one would hear him.

Gussie waves both hands at us, almost as if we're a flock of birds devouring her garden.

There's nothing we can do. We back out and stand near the door. Kids are still leaving: Becca with a bruise like an apple on her knee. And is that her partner?

He looks familiar. Messy dark hair...

"Alex," Zack whispers. "The new principal's son."

He looks worn out, wearing shorts that show his black-and-blue shins. He's bent over, trying to catch his breath.

I'm glad Zack and I go in for easier sports, climbing eight-foot toothpick trees, carrying ten-ton books around, digging up lawns.

A few more kids straggle out, then Gussie herself. She locks the door and heads for her car.

Zack, Yulefski, and I throw ourselves down in front of the cellar window, trying to peer in. "Steadman," I whisper loudly.

Yulefski stuffs most of her fingers into her mouth, then wipes the filthy glass. Pretty disgusting, if you ask me, but she's given us a better view of the window with its bite-sized hole. "Hmm," she says. "That reminds me of something. But what?"

We peer down into a black hole. All we can see are shadows. One of the shadows is waving his arms at us. "I can't get out!" Steadman wails. He sounds far away. He also sounds desperate.

We're desperate, too.

Chapter 21

We crouch against the damp window, talking to Steadman, trying to make him feel better.

"I'll be here forever," he moans.

Yulefski leans her head against the small opening. "No, just for a couple of hours."

Steadman screams louder than the train that's pulling in on the other side of the tracks. "Hours? That's forever."

Zack gives Yulefski an angry *zip the lip* with his finger.

"Don't worry," I tell Steadman, "we'll bring you food, anything you like. We'll just hand it down through the window."

Zack glares at me as if I'm almost as bad as Yulefski.

"It's dark in here!" Steadman screams.

There's no help for it. Somehow we have to get in there and rescue him.

Zack puts his mouth up close to the window. "Just count to a thousand..."

"Slowly," Yulefski puts in.

"I can't even count to a hundred!" Steadman yells.

From the corner of my eye, I see a guy coming around the corner, swinging a pail and a mop. He clunks down the pail, reaches into his pocket, and pulls out a bunch of keys.

In the background, I hear Steadman: "Fourteen, fifteen, seventeen..."

"Sixteen," Yulefski says.

I take a breath and head for the door. "Hey, mister!" I yell.

"Twenty-eight..."

The man turns.

"I left some stuff in there," I say.

He raises his shoulders in the air. "Sure."

It's as easy as that. I follow him inside and head for the cellar door as he whistles his way down the hall and disappears around a corner.

"Hang on, Steadman," I whisper to myself. "You're saved."

Almost.

The cellar door is locked.

What to do? I go back down the hall. How can I ask the guy for a key?

But there's a miracle: a set of keys on Gussie's desk, just waiting to be scooped up...

...which I do in a hurry.

In my mind I can almost hear Steadman counting.

I go downstairs; it gets darker with every step. "I'm here," I call, and fall over boxes and nets trying to reach him.

He trips over metal bats and tennis rackets. We reach out to each other in the dark.

"I thought I'd never see you again," he tells me.

"I'd always come and get you."

"I keep whispering that same thing to Fred," he says. "Sometimes he can read my mind."

I hear the mop-and-pail guy; a door slams.

What now?

The cellar door. I forgot to close it.

I grab Steadman's hand. Together we go up the stairs. I give the door a push, but it doesn't budge. Not only has the whistler closed it, he's locked it, too. We're probably in here until the morning. At least. And the only light is a thin wedge coming from under the door.

Steadman still doesn't realize what's going on. "Wait a minute," I tell him. "I want to investigate the rest of the basement."

"I heard something crawling around in the corner before," Steadman says. "Probably a rat."

"Probably a cricket," I tell him. "You love crickets."

Down we go, back into the dark, into the rats' domain . . . or worse. Except I can't think of anything worse.

I look up at the window; I see Zack's back and Yulefski's. "Hey!" I yell.

"That must be Hunter at the door," Zack says. "Let's go."

"Don't go!" I yell.

Too late.

They're gone, around to the front.

Steadman's beginning to realize that we're still trapped.

I'm beginning to realize that rats' teeth are like razors, and that I couldn't find socks to put on this morning. I'm beginning to realize I'm terrified.

Above me, someone is rattling the window. I look up and cringe. It's Bradley the Bully.

Steadman and I back up into the darkest corner. Even rats are friendlier than Bradley. What's he doing up there, anyway? He wiggles one bandaged finger into the bite-sized hole and snaps open the lock. "Leth go here," he tells himself.

Suddenly there's a hint of summer air, there's light. The window is open; Bradley crawls in and drops. He's two inches away from us and any rats that might be scurrying around.

I put my hand over Steadman's mouth. But Bradley brushes right past us. He heads for the stairs. What a surprise he's going to get when he reaches the door.

But no surprise.

He must have a key.

The door opens, closes, and he's gone.

"What's he doing here, anyway?" Steadman asks.

"Playing basketball, or something, without paying the six bucks," I answer.

We wait awhile; then we tiptoe up the stairs and into the hall.

We hear Bradley shooting hoops: *ba-boom, ba-boom;* we edge our way down the hall without making a sound. The whistler is asleep on a couch in the coatroom, his pail and mop propped up against the wall.

"We're out of here," I tell Steadman.

But wait.

I back up.

"Come on, Hunter," Steadman says. "I'm starving to death."

I raise my hand, hardly paying attention to him. I stare at that picture of a cat taped up behind the desk. I stare at a picture of a dog.

I stare at the words: **HUGE PRIZES**.

I pull Steadman around to the back of the desk. And I see it. I really see it.

BRING YOUR PET. TEACH HIM GYMNAS-TICS. ALMOST FREE. PRIZES FOR THE WIN-NERS, ESPECIALLY SIX DOLLARS TUITION!

I read it again and say it aloud, trying to put it together.

"Fred would be great at gymnastics," Steadman says, still sniffling.

"You're right." I stare at something else: a list of dogs, cats, and their names, all entered into the gymnastics contest.

I run my finger down the list. There are a bunch of Buddys, a couple of Pals, two Fluffys, and one Frederika.

Frederika?

Could it be?

But there's no time to think. I hear something. Bradley? The whistler? Rats coming up the stairs?

"Let's go," I tell Steadman, and we run like antelopes right out the door.

Chapter 22

We head for home and slide into the kitchen. Mom is upstairs with K.G. and Mary. Too bad she doesn't just relax and come down for dinner. Nana's Pineapple Chicken isn't half-bad.

"Your father's gone to Acme Hardware Store," Nana says. "He's given up on the lawn. He wants to build a porch out back, but his boards and nails are missing."

Zack gulps. I stare down at my plate. I root around, pushing the weedy greens to one side, and take a mouthful of pineapple. I chew slowly. I have to concentrate.

Zack isn't concentrating. He's wolfing down the chicken as if he hasn't had a meal in a week. "Let's go, Hunter," he says.

"What about all those books in the living room?" Linny says.

"We're building a ladder with them," Zack tells her. "Right to the ceiling."

Linny rolls her eyes at Nana. "I'll probably have to take them back to the library myself."

"Good work, Linny," Zack says.

I follow him out the door, with Steadman behind us. That's all we need.

"Listen, Steadman," Zack says. "You have to guard the house. Keep watching in case something comes up about Fred."

Steadman's lips go out about a mile. "What could come up?"

I lean forward, trying to think. "Suppose the kidnapper walks by with him?"

Steadman leans forward.

"Keep an eye on the living room window," I say.

Steadman nods. "I'll do it."

Across the street in Werewolf Woods, Zack and I sink down and lean against one of the toothpick trees. Zack chews on a blade of grass. I chew on my nails.

"So who is it?" Zack asks.

"Someone who belongs to the gym. Someone who wants to enter Fred in the contest," Yulefski says from the next tree.

"Someone who knows how good Fred is at jumping and rolling around," Zack adds.

I have no nails left to chew. "Someone who needs six bucks to stay in the gym."

We look at each other. That's not William. William has tons of money.

Zack slaps his forehead. "Becca."

"Becca," Yulefski echoes.

I begin to shake my head. Isn't Becca afraid of Fred? Maybe not as afraid as she wants us to think.

I close my eyes. I rest my head against the tree. That's it! Becca. I see it in my mind: Becca bent over, pulling Fred along in the bag. Becca wearing a hat so no one will recognize her.

"What a weasel she is," Yulefski says.

Zack and I get to our feet. We have to go over to Becca's house right away. We march down the block, Yulefski right behind us. We dash across Murdock Avenue and end up at Becca's front path.

"Becca!" Zack yells.

"We want to talk to you!" I shout.

Yulefski adds an ear-piercing whistle.

But what do I see? Becca going out her back door, pulling a bag along behind her.

"Wait!" we all call together.

She doesn't wait. Does she even hear us? She slams the bag over her cyclone fence into the next yard. Poor Fred, his brains must be scrambled.

Next Becca throws herself over the fence. She's heading for Suicide Hill. We climb over her fence a moment later. The top edges are sharp enough to amputate our fingers.

Becca runs like a cheetah; so does Yulefski. Zack and I huff and puff behind them. We have no breath to yell at her. Becca's bag jostles from one side to the other.

And there's Suicide Hill, looming up in front of us.

Becca stops. She reaches into the bag. She holds it upside down.

Oh, Fred.

What falls out is definitely not Fred. It's a skateboard.

She's probably killed him already with her rough treatment!

"Hold it right there, Becca!" Yulefski yells.

Becca doesn't hold it. With the bag floating out behind her, she skates down Suicide Hill.

We race after her, the cement coming up to meet our sneakers. We'll never get to the end alive. We'll have to be buried on the front lawn. It's a good thing there's plenty of room under the gravestone.

Zack falls first, and I'm right after him. We roll over and over, cement messing up our hands, our knees, our faces.

But Becca sails on, with Yulefski right behind her, catching up, ready to grab her. "Where's the body?" Yulefski shouts, and spins her around.

We get to our feet.

"Body?" Becca yells, clutching her hair. "Someone's dead? Who is it?" She sinks down in the weeds next to the hill. "Probably Sister Appolonia. She's the oldest person I know."

Zack makes a Jell-O face. "Maybe Becca's not the kidnapper," I say.

"Kidnapper?" Becca yells. "Has Linny been kidnapped? I didn't believe her when she told me."

Yulefski runs her teeth over her Rice Chex–filled braces. "You didn't kidnap Fred?"

Becca's still yelling. "Not Sister Appolonia? Not Linny?"

"Fred," I say.

Becca slaps her head. "Who'd steal that dog?"

We all look at each other.

We don't have a clue.

DOOMSDAY . . .
MINUS ONE

We're dragging ourselves . . .

Chapter 23

. . . to the classroom where we'll spend the rest of the year in captivity.

We're trying to think of books we might have read before Sister Appolonia gets hold of us.

"There was that girl," Zack says. "Something about a pest?"

"We used her in a report last year," I say. "Or maybe the year before. Or maybe even—"

"There's always that spider, or the kid on the prairie." Zack snaps his fingers. "And what about that rabbit hole business?"

I shake my head. Did we read all that?

And there's Yulefski again, leaning against the brick wall, reading. She waves three fingers at us.

Sister Appolonia stands at the head of the stairs. She's not interested in our reading right now. She's interested in our dragging a hundred books up from the storeroom and moving her thousand-pound desk from one side of the room to the other. She's interested in our washing the chalkboard, dusting the tables, and watering the half-dead plants, while she disappears somewhere.

We're standing at the windowsill, taking a rest, when we spot the new kid, Alex, coming out of the used-to-be-empty house. He's pulling along a Gussie's Gym bag that moves, and sways, and bulges.

Bent over like an old man, the kid sneaks across the street. But now something is happening to the bag; it's growing a hole. What appears is a brown weasel face with a set of choppers that are sharper than the teeth of the rats in Gussie's basement.

Fred!

The kid turns and sees what's going on in the bag as Fred wiggles out and heads for home.

"Go, boy!" Zack and I yell together.

The kid gives chase, and the two of them dash across the school lawn.

We shove up the window and poke our heads out as far as we can, but we can't see where they are.

There's only one thing to do. We climb out on the ledge, which is about four inches wide, and teeter there, two stories up, yelling, "Stop, thief!"

The kid looks up at us and keeps going around the corner. We keep going, too...

...along the ledge, holding on to the cement walls and the windows in between. We come to the corner, where we can see the schoolyard, the basketball hoop, the handball court.

Fred and the kid are at the next corner. Which way are they going?

"Hold on, feet," I tell myself. I lean out an inch, and then another.

My feet don't listen.

I feel it. I'm falling, my arms circling around like windmills. Zack's fingers pluck at my T-shirt.

Too late.

"Yeow!" Yulefski yells.

The wind whistles as I sail through the air, down and down, and at the last minute, grab...

...the basketball hoop.

I hang out in the wind with screws and bolts popping out of the hoop. Zack looks as if he's going to faint.

The kid stares up, mouth open. "Hang on!" he yells.

Fred sinks one of his choppers into the kid's ankle, and halfway across the street, Bradley the Bully stops, one foot in the air. "Amaathing!" he lisps, looking at me.

Sister Appolonia comes across the yard and stands under the hoop, arms out like giant hams. "Drop," she says in a voice not to be fooled with.

Another bolt pops. I close my eyes and let go. *"Yeeoooooow!"*

Oof. I'm folded into Sister Appolonia's arms. Above me,

Zack sits on the ledge, his face the color of the eggshells we feed the worms.

"Suppose you finish the classroom before the twenty-third century," Sister Appolonia suggests, and leaves me to catch my breath.

We're almost ready to work, but not yet. *"Komazahere!"* I yell.

Fred barrels toward me, doing somersaults, head over heels. He lands on my shoulders, takes a nip out of my neck, and wags what little tail he has.

"You're the kidnapper," I say to Alex.

He shakes his head. "I've been looking for a girl. I think she owns him. What's her name? Lillian? Lenore? Something like that."

"Linny!"

"Right. But I haven't seen her anywhere. I just rescued the dog from—" He breaks off and points.

And here comes Bradley, mooching himself across the street. "That wath thome dive," he lisps. I can hear the admiration in his voice.

Fred froths at the mouth as if he's going to tear Bradley to pieces.

I telescope myself to the fullest height I can manage. "I do lots of stuff like that," I say with a bully-type face.

Bradley takes a step back. "I wath going to borrow the dog for a couple of dayth," he says. "I wanted to win that animal conteth at Guthieth. Thikth buckth, you know? I'm tired of pulling the window in and out every night."

"Thickth!" a voice says behind us. It's Yulefski, of course. "That's it! He meant *six*! It's the voice I heard in Vinny's Vegetables. He must have been talking to himself. And the third clue, the hand, the bandage." She looks as if she's solved the mystery single-handed.

Sure.

I turn to Bradley.

Zack comes along in time to hear me warn him. "Don't give us any more trouble," I say, knees trembling. "Otherwise..." I run my finger across my throat. "Toast!"

"Yeah," Zack says from behind me.

Bradley nods earnestly. "Don't worry."

Zack and I finish cleaning the classroom with one detour. We deliver Fred to Steadman, who is overjoyed.

For once, Linny smiles at us. "As Steadman would say, *notobado*," she says.

Only one problem is left. We have to read three books that will change our lives in less than a day.

THIS IS IT!
DOOMSDAY!

In case anyone forgot.

Chapter 24

Mom stands at the front door with K.G. in her arms and Mary leaning against her legs. "Bye-bye," Mary calls; Mom smiles at us and waves. Pop is smiling, too. He loves the first day of school. K.G. just screams, but that's all right; she's looking good.

We head down the street together, Linny, William, Zack, me, and Steadman for the first time. Fred follows until Steadman gives him a *"Gozahome."* Fred turns, skinny tail down, and trots back to the front door.

Next to me, Linny smells like perfume. It's from the A. Ransom Company. Becca gave it to her for an early birthday present. "Everyone is getting some," Becca says. "Didn't your mother get the letter? This is the one."

She waves the letter around.

I look down at it. *Kids: Want to look like more than $1,000,000? Different from all the others? Line up from attic to cellar. Try New You Perfume from the A. Ransom Company.*

There's more, but I don't bother to read the rest. It's definitely the kidnap letter.

Sheesh.

"Actually, it's not so bad to go back to school," Zack says, and yawns.

I yawn, too. We've been up all night, reading. Sentence after sentence. Page after page. Amazing. The books we brought home were all about worms.

Everyone else was up all night, too. K.G. sleeps about twenty minutes at a time. Then Mary chimes in. Fred barks whenever anyone goes near Steadman's door at night. He's not going to be kidnapped a second time.

But I'm thinking about the worm books. Did they change our lives? Maybe not yet, but soon. We're entering the worms in the Gussie's Gym Pet Contest. They squirm, they wiggle. They actually might do backflips.

I think they have a chance at winning.

I look back at Werewolf Woods and the pond. Bradley says it's a great fishing spot. He's been scaring everyone away, but because Zack and I are so tough, he's invited us to go with him.

Maybe we'll catch something.

Maybe not.

We go to school, happy.

But then . . .

Instead of reading, we have to write what we did during our summer vacation.

Boring.

Actually, we didn't do anything. We might have to make the whole thing up. A work of fiction, as Sister Appolonia would say.

About the author

Patricia Reilly Giff is the author of many highly acclaimed books for children, including *Lily's Crossing,* a Newbery Honor Book and *Boston Globe*–Horn Book Honor Book, *Pictures of Hollis Woods,* a Newbery Honor Book; and *Don't Tell the Girls: A Family Memoir.* An avid reader as a child she was also a reading teacher in New York City public schools for twenty years. She writes, "All of my books are based in some way on my personal experiences, or the experiences of members of my family, or the stories kids would tell me in school." She now lives in Connecticut with her husband Jim.